The CULLEN books by Mark Farrer (in chronological order):

Dirty Barry

Where Seagulls Dare

Bronchial Billy

A Fistful Of Collars

Pale Ale Rider

The Good The Bad & The Rugby

DIRTY BARRY

mark farrer

funny business press

DIRTY BARRY

ISBN: 978-1-9164892-4-0

Published by Funny Business Press

To Paul
For putting up with it.

This is a work of fiction.
Names, characters, places and incidents either are products of the author's imagination or are used fictitiously.
Any resemblance to actual events or locales or persons, living or dead, is entirely coincidental .
Except for Big Paul.

CONTENTS

PART ONE

THE TOOTH

ONE

The man in the cowboy hat stood in the shop doorway trying not to stand on the cheese.

"Come in! Shut the door." Archie fussed. "Not quite open yet." Cullen closed the door behind him and slid into the shop, surveying the interior: shelves still being stocked, half-unpacked cardboard boxes scattered across the floor. Cheeses, large and small, everywhere.

"Mind!" Archie warned as Cullen dripped onto the newly-laid wooden flooring. He was wearing a battered leather cowboy hat, currently dark brown, saturated as it was with heavy rain donated gratis by the Scottish Borders weather. His waterproof was a dirty lime green, with a rip in one shoulder and heavy stain below the right pocket; similarly rain-soaked camo pants clung to his legs and dripped onto the tops of brown leather walking boots that had seen better days. He stood there, staring into the middle-distance - like a horse taking a long piss - while Archie weighed him up.

Cullen stood a smidge over six foot with a relaxed, muscular ease and a detached bearing. The clothes might have said shambolic but the stance and gait told a different story. His grey eyes were alert and sparkled in the thin overhead lighting and, as he turned his head to scan the shop, Archie could see a broken nose, clean jawline and strong forehead, creased and lined; few laughter lines around the eyes. Wisps of salt-and-pepper hair curled untidily beneath the brim of his hat which was jammed onto his head rather unceremoniously, forcing his ears outward so that they stuck out rudely.

"Come through, come through!" Archie waved Cullen into the back room, peering out through the window nervously. On the counter was a large wodge of paper carrier bags, still wrapped in cellophane, which bore the legend: *A B Cheese Ltd* and underneath, in a different font, *Goodness Graters Me.*

The two men passed into a narrow corridor which turned sharply left then right and opened out into a dark, cold space with walls of bare brick and stone. Archie threw the switch which jolted four strip-lights high above them into stuttering life. They illuminated a large storeroom containing several rows of slatted wooden racks, tiered from floor to ceiling, some fifteen feet high. The racks were arranged down the room like shelves in a library, with space to move between each one and a ladder at each end to allow access to the top two or three sets of shelves. Each shelf was full of rounds, wheels, cubes, slabs and enormous portions of cheese.

Cullen scanned the setup and wrinkled his nose at the rank mixture of aromas infiltrating his nostrils.

"What do you think, hmm?" Archie gestured proudly, surveying his stock. "Best selection of cheeses North of the border by a mile. Thousands of pounds' worth here in the room. Thousands!"

"Huh." Cullen said.

Archie scowled and busied himself with the loose ends of a string which had been holding a set of Jarlsberg wheels together in a pile. He was a small, delicate man, with narrow face and dark-brown eyes, and a shock of grey hair which almost stood on end. This, combined with his rapid movements, made him look a bit like a Great Crested Grebe. He looked around at Cullen, curious.

"Where's your... weapon?"

"Don't do weapons." Cullen shrugged, scanning the storeroom. "What's here?"

Archie's face fell and a sudden panic gripped him. "You never said that!" He looked Cullen up and down, worried. "Hand-to-hand combat, is that it?"

"Last resort." Cullen huffed, pulling himself up onto one of the ladders and testing the sturdiness of the ceiling-height rack.

"Great." Archie put his hands on his hips. "Mr Resourceful then, is it? This is my livelihood we're talking about here!"

"Be fine." Cullen answered, eyes creased in thought. "Any other exits?"

"Be fine? Listen, if you can't catch this bloke, I may as well not open for business at all! No, the one we've just come in through and that back door there, all there is." Archie pointed to a black wooden door bearing a large Fire Exit sign. "That's the way he must be getting in and out. Got an alarm out front. Fitter's coming back Tuesday to do this back one."

"Hmm." Cullen looked down from his perch onto Archie. "Should have got 'em done the other way round."

"Yeah. Thanks, Mister Hindsight. Look, none of this is... my area of expertise. My area of expertise is cheese!"

"Hmm." Cullen repeated, absently, sucking his teeth in thought. "Maybe we can use your expertise then."

"What, you gonna do? Kill him with a cheese?"

"No-one said anything about killing anyone." Cullen, his face now five shelves up off the floor, prodded a large cheese wheel in front of him. "How heavy are these things?"

"If you did - it'd be a cheese topping! Geddit?" Archie looked up to see if Cullen had caught his joke and then howled in protest. "Hey, don't do that! That's Cornish Yarg. You damage the nettle covering and people won't buy it."

"How heavy?"

"Depends." Archie sighed. "These here..." he waved at a rack beside him. "Smaller ones: four, five kilos for the Goudas or Bries, up to maybe nine or ten for the large ones like the Lancashire or Stilton."

"What's that in old money?"

"Anywhere from ten to twenty pounds. Weight." Archie added.

"What about this one?" Cullen picked up a large grey cylinder and gave it some thoughtful heft.

"That's a soft cheese. Not sure you could kill someone with soft cheese, could you?"

"I told you - there's no killing here. What's your biggest one?"

"Ooh, that'll be the Cheddars down the back there. Forty, forty-five kilos I think. Ninety-odd pounds." Archie converted helpfully.

"Christ!" Cullen grimaced. "Not sure I could lift that."

"You don't have to lift it, do you? Can't you just push it off the shelf?"

Cullen had stopped listening and moved over to another rack.

"This one?"

"Parmigiano-Reggiano. Beautifully complex. Nearly forty kilos. You can't use that! Sell that in small portions, it's worth nearly a grand. You'll put me out of business!"

"Thought that was this other guy's job." Cullen moved

along the shelves, poking and prodding the mouldy rinds of cheeses, while Archie winced below.

When the handle on the back door first twitched, Cullen was lying on the top tier of shelving in the dark, his chin resting on his arms crossed in front of him. Archie was hunkered down behind a stack of empty packing crates in the far corner with a perfect view of the door.

There was a scratching and ratcheting sound and then the lock gave suddenly. A balaclava'd head appeared around the door, silhouetted in the lights from the alley outside. The head waited half a minute, cocked slightly, before quickly glancing back and then ducking inside and closing the door behind it. The light in the room shrank further and the figure paused once again, perhaps waiting for his eyes to adjust.

Archie crouched motionless, holding his breath. He looked up to Cullen's perch but found he was no longer there. His eyes scoured the room, ears pricked for the slightest sound. All was still and quiet.

The intruder stepped lightly forward two paces and turned his head to the side, as if looking straight into Archie's eyes. He turned his head away again and took one more step forward, before being flattened by forty-five kilos of Cheddar. Extra Mature.

Cullen jumped down from nowhere and stood over the fallen figure. He reached out with his right boot to nudge the body on the floor and Archie unfolded himself from his hiding place and reached for the light switch.

"Yay! Nice work. Though was hoping you'd have gone for the Double Gloucester. Cheaper." He screwed his eyes up as the strip-lights blinked on, just as the figure on the floor lashed out with one leg. Cullen collapsed on his coccyx, yelling out in pain and surprise.

"Shit!" As the figure in the balaclava struggled to his knees, rubbing its shoulder, Archie reached to his left for anything he could grab. His hand found half a wheel of his finest Gorgonzola Piccante, £16 per kilo, and he reluctantly launched it at the head of the intruder. The cheese sailed past the man and splattered against the far wall, leaving blue-veined chunks stuck to the painted breeze-block.

Cullen was now back on his feet and he leapt at the figure in black, knocking them both to the ground. They wrestled briefly until Archie's fingers found a ball of eighteen-month old Gouda, pristine in black and gold foil. He closed his eyes, unable to accept he was throwing good money and fantastic cheese at a stranger, before gritting his teeth and hurling the missile at the tussling pair.

The cheese smacked Cullen squarely on the jaw, knocking his hat off with the impact

"Ow, fuck!" Cullen lost his grip on the intruder who squirmed back to his feet and lurched for the door. "Help me out, Archie! Fuck sake!"

Archie flicked the lights off again and tried as stealthily as he could to make his way round to the back door and cut off the intruder's escape. Cullen flailed blindly for the stranger and caught his heel, sending him skittering off-balance and slamming hard into the shelving to his right.

It started to rain small pieces of cheese.

Cullen hurled himself into the stomach of the man, now defending himself from an attack of Danish Blues, Babybels and smaller Edams that hailed down on him from above. The pair grappled and bounced along the shelving unit, like paired ball-bearings in some demented pinball machine, each impact showering more discs of Camembert, Cambozola and Brie down to earth.

Cullen had a clear height and strength advantage over the chubbier compact figure in the balaclava who skidded on a Blue D'Auvergne and fell to his knees. Cullen reached for the nearest cheese he could grasp and round-housed it into the man's face, delivering the *coup de gras*. The intruder slumped unconscious to the floor and Archie threw the lights back on and hurried over to Cullen. On his knees, panting raggedly, Cullen dropped the bloody, mashed cheese weapon to the floor.

Archie let out a plaintive cry. "My Stinking Bishop!"

Cullen looked up at him, testing his lower jaw. "You're welcome." He got to his feet and retrieved his hat, planting it roughly back on his sweat-soaked head. "Who is it then?"

"Hmm?" Archie was surveying the carnage that had been his cheese storeroom, his face etched with sadness and dismay. "Look at it! Just... look at it."

"I'll do the honours then, shall I?" Cullen strode over to the figure on the floor, bent down and peeled back the balaclava.

"Simpson!" Exclaimed Archie, looking at the unconscious man's swollen face.

"You know him, then?"

"Runs the deli down the High Street." Archie spat. "Bastard! So that's his game, is it? Damaging and stealing my stock, trying to put me out of business before I even open. Huh, business must be bad." He cast his eyes glumly over the floor. It was littered with several smashed wheels of cheese, some stamped on, one flattened. Cheese shrapnel everywhere. "Guess he was scared of competition. Going to struggle myself now, all this damaged stock." He strode over to the unconscious figure and aimed a sharp kick in the man's ribs. "Take that, you bastard! I hope your business goes down the toilet, where it belongs."

"Steady." Cullen said, raising his eyebrows.

"Don't steady me. That's who you've got to blame for a sore mouth."

"Well, no. Technically, that was you."

"Fine. Whatever."

"And it hurts." Cullen cradled his mouth and tentatively waggled his jaw.

"Well, that's all very well and good but what about my shop? I'm opening in two days." Archie held himself close with both arms and frowned at Cullen. "What about all this?"

Cullen ignored the damage in the room, nursing his mouth. "Still hurts."

"Are you serious?" Archie glared at him. "Look at it! I'll be able to salvage these hard cheeses. I guess. Cut off the dinged and dirty sections and leave the clean stuff for sale. But this softer stuff - it's flattened. Or ruined. Who's going to want to eat any of this?"

Cullen shrugged. "I will."

"Well you're fucking welcome to it." Archie snapped. "Here."

He scooped up the mashed wheel of Stinking Bishop, shoved it into Cullen's hands, and then bent to the task of picking all the salvageable pieces off the floor. Cullen watched Archie go about his business for a while, then stuffed the cheese into his rucksack and slunk out of the room, head down.

PART TWO

THE BLUETOOTH

TWO

Barry Sullivan's dental surgery in Peebles was a modern, brightly-lit affair with blonde wood, pastel carpets and not a tropical fish in sight. On the ground floor of a modern office block, the front door opened onto a large reception area, seats along three sides of a rectangle with a wall and inset glass screens along the fourth, behind which sat the receptionists: gatekeepers to hallowed pain relief.

From here, a long corridor led down the central spine of the surgery with three separate rooms leading from it, each the dedicated nest of one of the resident dentists: Michael Willingham, Sally Richards and Barry himself. The whole surgery reeked of the hushed tones of the church - ironic, really, Barry always considered, since what a dentists actually needed was some significant background noise to drown out the sounds of whining drills, grinding sanders or the intermittent cries of pain from protesting patients. A respectful hush hung over proceedings - from the customers themselves, silently supplicating in the waiting area, through the soothing plainsong of the novice receptionists on the phones, to the whispering chapel of uniformed dental assistants quietly shuffling like a choir of Clarins-clad nuns.

Novices and nuns. Always women. Barry made sure of that.

He watched Alison rule front of house like an angry

tamarind monkey protecting her fruit from a marauding chimp, but insisted that he personally vet new receptionists or dental assistants as the final step in the recruitment process. She may have excelled at placing adverts, perusing CVs, arranging and conducting interviews - but that counted for nothing if a candidate had a small chest, thin lips or was likely to refuse him a quick feel at the end of a hard day.

And days were hard. Or at least, that's how it felt when you were staring into the stinking abyss of bad dental work seven hours a day. The mask helped, of course, but the constant reminder of poor oral care, and the probing and tutting over past scars of repairs done in the dark, barbaric ages of 20th century dentistry - they all took their mental toll. Come 5pm, what Barry needed most of all was a damn good shag. Or blowjob at least. Something that would cleanse his mind and clear the custard.

He had started this dental practice from the ground up five years ago, having moved from an over-crowded practice on the other side of town, and brought many of his patients with him. The upside of taking on NHS patients had been a quick growth to capacity in terms of patient numbers; the downside had been the quality and opportunity for custard-clearing available to him. So he had applied himself with a steady focus and changed it.

Because Barry was nothing if not focussed. And his goal was now extra-marital sex.

In fact, it was extra-marital on both sides. Not for him, the pursuit and capture of innocent single women whose cavities he could probe. He wanted the thrill of more mature women - married, sexually accomplished and, not to put too fine a point on it, more at ease with the idea that a man might press and demand so that a woman would acquiesce and comply. Not for him these modern women who would cry harassment the minute you looked them up and down admiringly; he had no time for innocents who had had fewer partners than they had untrimmed pubic hairs.

When Julia McInnes initially walked into his surgery, Barry's eyes bulged noticeably. *Jesus suffering fuck*, she was gorgeous! He mentally reviewed her file that he'd seen for the first time that morning:

39 years old, married (natch). Perfect dental health record, no allergies. X-rays on file from her previous dentist showed a good set of top and bottom teeth. Hygienist records showed good alignment, no discolouration or gum issues, and evidence of excellent personal hygiene and oral care.

Barry's own ideas of Julia's oral care gave him a momentary throb in his pants. He watched her as she entered the room and manoeuvred herself into his leather dentist chair. She was tall and slim, long legs and shapely calves showing beneath a fairly demure knee-length skirt and navy blue woollen coat, which she had shed and sloped carefully on the guest chair by the door. Her legs were bare, smooth and wore the remains of a tan. She had a mole by her right ankle.

Her hands were slender with long fingers, nails polished expertly in a glittering blue. She wore a small diamond engagement ring, a simple gold wedding band and no other jewellery. On her left wrist was a thin silver-strapped watch with an analog face; on her right was a pale blue Fitbit.

Her hair was an auburn bob, short and thick with a

feathered edge which framed her oval face. Her brown eyes sparkled with good humour and warmth and her eyebrows looked like she had had them recently plucked. She wore pale pink lip gloss above a pixie chin, but the laugh-lines around her eyes gave her a more wearisome expression when up-close.

As he reclined the chair and moved the lamp over her face, he watched as her blouse shifted and the slight swelling of her breasts was revealed as the chair reached the horizontal. When she opened her mouth he could see beautiful healthy teeth, moist pinkness and a small tongue.

With a stud in it. Barry's pants throbbed again.

"Any issues or concerns about your teeth, Mrs McInnes?" He ran his tongue over his front teeth and smiled encouragement. He thought he could detect her eyes widening.

"No. I'm good." Julia replied confidently.

"Yes. Yes, you are." Breathed Barry, and fumbled awkwardly for his dental pick.

"So, I think that back tooth there perhaps needs some further investigation. Other than that everything looks fine. Better than fine, in fact. Excellent!" Barry pulled back his stool on castors and raised Julia slowly back up to a sitting position in the chair. "I'm a bit pushed for time right now. But I do have free slots later in the week - if you could pop in for an x-ray and a closer look."

Julia looked doubtful. "Well, I'm only five minutes away but I do have an awful lot on this week."

"Well it would probably only take five minutes." Barry breezed. "Tell you what. Ask reception on the way out for a 5pm appointment. I always have a bit of free time then and they'll know it's ok to squeeze you in if you tell them that."

"Right. Ok." Julia swung her legs beautifully over and stood up, heels clicking on the tiled floor as she put on her coat.

"Super. Well, it's a date then!" Barry gave a broad grin and Julia smiled shyly in return. She picked up her handbag and tottered wonderingly out of the surgery.

Paul McInnes was known to everyone, even his wife, as Big Paul. She alone had an intimate knowledge of "little Paul" as well - and even that was big. Big Paul was often shortened to B.P which was itself, again, shortened to Beep. A nickname which, ironically, measured up poorly against the scale of the man it described. Paul was a man mountain. Six foot five and eighteen stone, broad and wide, heavyset and muscular, with a bull's neck, an ox's chest and forearms like Popeye's bench-press nemesis.

Paul and Julia lived in a 3-bedroom semi on a new-build estate on the south-eastern edge of Peebles. Built on land that used to be part of a farm - until the farmer realised he could retire from rearing meagre livestock grazing on crap soil and exchange it for the simple pleasures of tarmac, driveways and money in the bank.

In some aspects of life, Paul was a master. He was, for instance, an excellent carpenter and a practical hands-on sort who could fix or knock up a solution to anything if it involved wood, screws or nails. Or glue. Paul was big on glue. Some things may be beyond him: literature, physics, tact. Others came naturally to him: heft, strength, practical ingenuity. Today, though, had seemed to involve Paul in an almighty helping of something he was appalling at - and always had been: punctuality.

When he was a boy, being on time had been uncool. Profoundly uncool. Coolness was denoted by a swaggering insouciance and don't-care attitude in the face of foolish teachers and their hysterical demands for homework. Paul withstood them all. And if it involved getting six of the best, trousers down, so be it. All that would do would ratchet up the cool factor. Plus liking school - I mean, actually liking it? Major minus coolness points for that alone. Not giving a shit, made major league sense. So that is what he did.

To many of his classmates, Paul seemed to have it all. Alas, once adulthood and the world of work beckoned, the pinnacle of cool swiftly melted into a puddle of mediocrity. Paul, with his natural Panglossian outlook, tried to swan serenely through it, brow unfurrowed by worry, uncreased by doubt. Bish-bash-bosh, job done and on to the next one. Next week would take care of itself once it became this week. You could worry about it, or not worry about it - made no odds. So, the easiest approach seemed to be to not worry about it. So Paul didn't.

And this lack of concern for earthly things, things that other mortals fretted over, could have - in other cultures, perhaps - made him something of a holy man. A sadhu, hermit, guru or seer. Someone who could sense beyond the material and value what was truly important and inescapable about life: its sheer brevity and glory. Revel in the now, worry not about whether your windows needed cleaning or your toilet was blocked. This was great wisdom - until you needed new front tyres and you had no money to pay for them, or you got a puncture on the M8 at midnight in a downpour.

So, time for Paul had a relativistic quality that Einstein

had identified but few others had genuinely grasped. Dilation it was not, but it certainly felt different for each participant. Paul would be there when he got there. For the waiting person, it was infuriating. And the fury was compounded when, in any attempt to explain to him why punctuality might be a good idea, Paul looked kindly at you as though you were clearly failing to grasp the larger, cosmic picture and say *Right, cool.*

And today, Paul was late. Relatively. With or without the nod to Einstein. Julia had told him, many times, that they were due at a dinner party at 8pm. And that, furthermore, a shower and change of clothes would be required of him as a minimum after he had been sanding solid oak flooring for eight hours straight. The invite had been extended to them by Stephen, Julia's boss, who owned the wholefoods distribution business she worked for. Julia, ever-ambitious, was angling for a promotion and this unexpected invitation had delighted her. This could be the break she needed and all Paul had to do was not fuck it up.

"Consider it done, my sweet." Paul's very words. "Which Steven was this again?" They knew a few Stevens.

"Stephen! You know! He always bangs on about it, Stephen with a 'ph'?"

"Phteven?"

Julia had clamped her jaw tight and glared at him. "Just. Don't. Be. Late".

It was 8:14pm when Paul's van pulled into the drive.

THREE

Julia loved Paul.

Or used to. Or still did? She asked herself this question daily and, daily, the answer changed.

Julia was bold and brassy, with a grin like Julia Roberts on acid and a laugh like a freshly unblocked drain. She could, and would, be the life and soul of the party at the drop of an ice cube in a Gin and Malibu - a Limbo Lady cocktail, her favourite. There was something just a little off-kilter about her features but her brown eyes glinted with a wickedness which was accentuated when she smiled, which she did a lot. She was tall, 5'10", and had spent a lifetime affecting a stoop for shorter boyfriends so that she never seemed to appear her full height, even in heels (which she had tended to avoid for the same reasons). Meeting Paul, a more than healthy 6'5" had meant for the first time she could hold her chin up, put on those heels, and not feel like some freak from Ringling Brothers Circus.

She hailed from the Isle of Sheppey, her father had worked at the Pool of London, before it had all been torn down and replaced with millionaire pads and Arab investment apartments. Her mother had been a translator in the Foreign Office, pouring over faxes and telexes day after day and translating communiques into diplomatic French in the days before the EU had accepted the universality of the English language with bad grace. Her father had loved her mother and Julia both - but left them anyway when she was barely into her teens. Having a wife who earned more than him, and had a higher social standing, ate away much of his pride and self-esteem. Dock closures and drinking away his redundancy pay took the rest. Julia clung to her mother and grew up reluctant to accept inferiority in male company, whilst eternally afraid that this very attitude would put paid to any chance of a long-term relationship. This, and her height, resigned her to singledom more often than she liked. So, as each year rolled by her standards lowered another notch.

Julia pretended to her girlfriends that she was more than delighted with her bachelor-career-girl status. She was a thrusting business-woman with deals to do and people to meet - she had no time for romance or children. Those could wait.

In the end, they waited far too long.

Eventually, and purely by accident, she had found herself migrating northwards to Edinburgh where she found a lover and boyfriend who happened to be the son of a wealthy farmer in the Scottish Borders. They had been planning a life together until one day she found him in the hay barn, *in flagrante* with one of his father's prize-winning ewes. Lowering standards or not, Julia had bolted from that relationship like a CEO with a plane to catch. On her last night at the Peebles Hydro, where she was attending a conference, she had been drowning her sorrows at the gin bar when she met Paul.

Paul was tall and olive-skinned, always wearing a beaming smile, with jet black hair cropped neatly to his large head and a short goatee which shone silkily. He was ubiquitous in the many pubs, bars and chippies that Peebles had to offer - it was even rumoured that he had black card membership of Greggs. And he was often to be found there in his working outfit of tatty old T-shirt, baggy grey jogging bottoms, and sweat-stained trainers. This despite the fact that work seemed to be something which often eluded him.

Or rather he eluded it.

Paul's attitude to work was one of benign tolerance. He enjoyed his job - he was a joiner by trade, and a very good one at that - but placed himself very much in the "work to live" camp, as opposed to the "live to work" one. His modus operandi for life was to coast along until money ran short - or out - and then rely upon the world to provide a job which would bring in some cash to allow this cycle to be repeated. And, truth be told, this worked out for him quite well. What might have infuriated and stressed many was, to Paul, a marvellous facet of life which he now took for granted. To any who would ever remark on the serenity and serendipity of his day-to-day existence, Paul would smile his broad smile, exposing glistening white teeth, tap the side of his nose theatrically and say "Trust the soup, mate. Trust the soup."

What he meant by this was, actually, known only to himself. But he said it with such confidence and conviction that everyone he said it to would just smile, think it was just Paul being Paul, and then ask about his dogs. And these three things - the soup and his two dogs - were the triumvirate of permanence on which Paul's existence rested.

His trusty Jack Russell terriers were called Penn and Teller. He had acquired them together as puppies when an old mate he had been doing a job for was short of readies to pay him and had suggested instead payment in kind - to whit, two cute puppies and a large dog basket. Charmed by their fluff and helplessness, Paul had agreed - knowing that the electricity would get paid some other way - and he had taken them home. Turn the clock forwards a few years and here they were, always by his side, as faithful, playful and fun-loving as Paul himself. Teller was the quiet one - large black and brown patches scattered over a mottled white coat with one ear that was constantly pricked and one which was not. Penn was a bouncy, yapping scoundrel who would steal your last sausage and then wag his tail at you, barking animatedly, whilst weighing you up with adoring eyes as if to say *Ok, so I nicked your last sausage, but I'm cute right?* He too had a mottled white coat with a single black patch which covered his front legs and chest.

And so it was, that Julia had seen Paul across the crowded bar. Mystically halo'ed somehow amidst the crush, like a prize ram being presented at auction. She had sized him up, assessing him for suitability in terms of size, smartness and looks. With only days to go before a friend's wedding she was due to attend with a plus-one she now didn't have, her quality benchmark was at an all-time low; Paul hurdled it with scant inches to spare. With the benefit of several gins under her belt, Julia had approached him and mercenarily extended her wedding invitation and the deal was quickly struck - almost as if Paul had no actual say in the matter - which was actually a state of affairs that suited him quite well.

The following weekend, at the end of the wedding reception, Julia and Paul had retired to the room she had booked for the night and they had balled each other's brains out 'til morning. There were complaints made at reception about the noise but when Julia had checked out later, with the shadowy hulking figure of Paul nuzzling her neck from behind, the manager had decided that discretion was the better part of valour and let the whole thing lie.

Alcohol may have had a large role to play in their successful date but, boy, was Paul sensational in the sack. Sure, her standards were temporarily low (and Prosecco seldom raised them) but he had strength, stamina, girth and heft where it counted. In fact, Julia had taken it upon herself to carefully scrutinise his girth and heft, once at close quarters with her eyes and hands, and twice with her mouth.

She had later compared notes with the no-longer blushing bride and discovered that their respective night-time experiences had been chalk and cheese, and that Julia had got by far the better of it. With the blindness that is lust, Julia became infatuated with Paul and the sexual delight he gave her. Weeks and months passed in a blur and they spent every second in each other's company that they could manage, sharing delight in each other's passions. And a wee personal mantra was born, one that Julia had recalled from an old childhood TV programme and which Paul too remembered when it first sprung, out of nowhere, to her lips:

Me and You, You and Me
Lots and lots for us to see
You and Me, Me and You
Lots and lots for us to do.

But as these things sometimes do, their romance blossomed only until the ardent nature of their coupling began to inevitably fade.

When Paul moved into Julia's flat, the practicalities, irritations and mundanities of life started to shape their lives more than their desires. And here it became apparent that for each and every facet of his magnificence in the bedroom department, Paul overcompensated by one or more corresponding failures in most other departments in the IKEA store of life. Grunting heavily, he would whistle aimlessly past the kitchen area, clog up the wardrobe and storage sections, ignoring home furnishings entirely before grinding to a complete halt at the checkout where actual money had to be exchanged.

Julia may have been an ambitious career woman, but her earnings were relatively small. She got by and was able to splash out now and then but it suddenly appeared as if she was now spending for two - on food, heating, petrol and so on - and not getting anything in the way of contributions other than the girth and heft that constituted Paul's payment in kind. He made a payment towards her rent but it was not always - scratch that, was never - on time and this was the start of Julia's frequent brushes with the maddening soup-trustiness that was Paul's stock-in-trade.

Within months, the grinding of teeth and gears in their relationship had started to bellow above the din of their intercourse. Which was when, entirely coincidentally, Paul had knocked her for six, charmed the socks off her and completely won her over when he asked her to marry him.

They say love is blind, and Julia had already decided that she was unsure whether she loved Paul or whether he was just so bloody loveable that it seemed that she did. He was fantastic and maddening in equal proportions and she realised that, since all individuals are flawed and none perfect, she should perhaps check the beam in her own eye before complaining about the mote in his. But above and beyond everything else - the lack of care with money, the vagueness, the undetectable work ethic - towering above all these, like some giant minaret in silver and gold, was his punctuality. Or lack of it.

It drove her completely nuts.

She tried to analyse it, reluctantly concluding that the sparks from *his* trait too often spat onto the scruffy hearthrug of *her* hang-up: being late. The result was never pretty.

It didn't matter whether it was business or pleasure - a meeting with a prospective customer or a dentist appointment - she became physically hot and sweaty, angry and ashamed, whenever she ran the risk of being late for anything. If she sat at the lights and calculated that she would be a few minutes late by the time she arrived, on came the hot flushes and the anxiety. And to the fore came her subconscious looking hungrily for someone or something to blame, that wasn't her: the weather, the traffic, the post, the prior appointment that had overrun. All would stand as she rolled them around in her mind's eye to see if they could justifiably be used as reasons for a possible late arrival, when all along she knew the basic truth was that she should take responsibility for her lateness by not cutting it so fine. She was a frustrated idealist - wanting the world to be perfect, making plans on the basis that it was, then becoming inevitably angry and disappointed when it turned out not to be and her plans collapsed in ruins. Rinse and repeat.

So Paul's approach to punctuality pushed all the wrong buttons for her and made her life intolerable whilst she sat there of an evening desperately trying to convince her inner voice that it was her, not him. But coming to the nightly conclusion that it was him and something must be done.

But what?

Julia loved Paul. Like a slug hates salt.

Paul loved Julia. Like a dog loves his master, like a child loves ice-cream, like a lawn loves the rain. As a sailor loves the sea, Paul relished life as it rose and fell beneath his feet, the breeze in his face and the horizon on the, erm, horizon. Nothing between here and there, so let's ride the tide to there and see what's there when we get there. Usually it was just more *there* that was there - but what the hell.

But just like a sailor needed shore leave to avoid going crazy, so Paul felt the deep draw of satisfaction when he found himself in a steady relationship. And found was a keyword here, as these things seemed to happen around him and he would wake up one morning and realise he was now part of a couple and was really quite delighted by his good fortune.

The stability and routine offered a steadiness and familiarity, cosiness and warmth like a wooden bowl of soup on a cold winter's day. It reinforced his view that life was good and the soup was to be trusted. Here was Julia: an attractive, shapely woman with a dirty laugh, smiling eyes and an excellent cook. She was resourceful, financially independent, enthusiastic and diligent and completely in love with his dick. Genuinely infatuated with it, it seemed. She sought it out whenever she could, sometimes looking to physically devour it as soon as it hove into view. There were many times when he actually wished she'd leave the bloody thing alone - and how many men would be able to say that? Or would be delighted to be in a similar position?

But there were a few times, he couldn't help but notice, when she grumped and moaned at him. Folded her arms and her mouth grew hard. He'd let her down, he guessed, but she wouldn't say why out loud and he didn't want to ask. So they steered a course from one bout of great sex to the next, by tacking into the wind: a repetitive, tiring practice of steering windward and feeling the boat and sails grow taut; straining under the tightness, until you needed to swing around and, in that moment of adjustment, everything grows slack and you have to smartly wrestle to regain that tautness to keep your momentum. Zig-zagging to a destination you couldn't reach in a straight line because that would require you to do the impossible: sail into the wind.

And that was their relationship - an uncharted journey to a hopeful destination which required them to constantly sail into the wind. For the five years of their marriage, each had tacked their own way, grew exhausted, only to reignite their energy in bed to give them the fight to tack once again the next day. While sharing a common goal and keeping their relationship on course, they nevertheless found the process exhausting and knew, deep down, that they couldn't maintain this effort indefinitely.

Something would have to give.

"Where have you been?" Julia, hands on hips, had been pacing and phoning, pacing and texting, pacing and calling Paul fit to burn at the top of her voice. She didn't want to sit down and crease her new frock. The frock that Paul hadn't noticed - no change there then.

Paul wondered what was wrong, saw his wife all dolled

up and mentally started to rappel back through the rickety rolodex in his mind for an engagement of some kind which might require dressing up. He came up empty. "Where're you off to?"

"What?" She instantly held up an angry hand to stifle the inevitable repetition of the question she knew Paul would utter. "Rhetorical. This-" she swept her hand down her outfit, ending with a blue nail-polished flourish. "Is what is called being ready for a dinner date. OUR dinner date. The dinner date with Stephen and Olivia I have been reminding you about over and over recently."

The fridge-door light in Paul's head winked on. "Um, yeah. Phteven?"

"The very same." She fumed. "Well?"

Paul looked at her, brows creasing. "Um."

"Where the fuck have you been? Why didn't you call to tell me you'd be late? And why aren't you fucking racing to the fucking shower this very fucking minute?"

"Is it now?"

"Get in the fucking shower you... arsehole!" Julia launched a failed kick at his backside as he slunk away towards the stairs.

"I'm going! I'm going!"

"I swear to God..." Julia picked up her phone and dialled Olivia, swallowing hard for a suitable apology.

When Paul came back downstairs he had a towel round his waist and was rubbing his hair dry with another. "What the fuck are you doing down here? Get back up those fucking stairs and get shaved and dressed pronto! No. Wait. Fuck the shave. Just get dressed. I've gained a thirty minute reprieve from Olivia, let's see if we can astonish her by getting there early, shall we?"

Paul, turned seamlessly on the stair and padded back

up, shaking his head slowly.

"I've left clothes out for you. On the bed!" Julia shouted at his back. "Don't touch anything else, just put those on and get back down here. Quickly!"

On the short walk home at the end of the night, Julia needled and jabbed at Paul trying to understand what had happened to cause him to be late. She knew it was pointless. Either he had forgotten all about it, never remembered in the first place, or didn't care. Either way, it was all too evident after years of marriage that Paul clearly could not be relied upon to turn up when needed. Inherently unreliable - her mother's words when she had first met him. Actually, no, her first words had described Paul as being something like a cross between a hoover and a head injury. Whatever.

Julia wasn't sure how her mother had been able to come to that conclusion so rapidly, and back in those days when her head had been turned by this magnificent specimen of masculinity, Julia had defended Paul proudly. These few years later, as her heels clacked on the frosty paving stones, she realised bitterly that her mother had been right, and Paul was never going to change. Her choice was to accept that and love him. Or not.

And after tonight's debacle she was sliding inexorably into the *not* camp. It was all too late for recriminations, she was just going through the motions: the tediously inevitable marital game where the arguments changed each time but the underlying issue remained constant. The evening had been a disaster and it was all she could do to stop herself from getting into a brawl with him right there, in the freezing night air. There was to be no promotion.

Probably not ever now. The anger and betrayal roiled within her, stoked by a feeling of utter powerlessness over her own future.

Paul slouched along in silence beside her, bent beneath a silent barrage of outrage and bitter disappointment. At the end of their driveway, Julia stopped and let Paul shuffle to the door and open it. He looked back and held the door open, quizzically for a second or two and then, seeing she was not moving, gently left it ajar and disappeared upstairs. Julia looked up at the stars for a few moments, saw their bedroom light come on and then hung her head and let the tears finally come.

FOUR

Barry "Beaver" Sullivan had a stiff neck and a dead arm. He woke, bleary-eyed and thick-headed, lying on the carpet in front of a looping Blu-ray menu on a large TV screen with the sound off.

It was Monday, 5.30am.

In a few hours' time he had to be at work, and this evening he had a room booked at his usual hotel in Edinburgh where he would be entertaining his latest Stepford Wife. Dealing with the hurt pride of his own wife, Melinda, could wait. It wasn't the first time, and it wouldn't be the last. Maybe it could wait forever. He, on the other hand, noticing a budding morning glory rising in his trousers, could not.

His weeks didn't usually start like this. Sometimes, but not usually. Last night had not been unusual in that he had had a row with his wife, and let her stomp upstairs to bed while he finished off the bottle of Pinot Grigio. They hadn't even got to the end of the film before the argument broke out. That wasn't unusual either.

Neither was the fact that the row had been about money. Because it was always about money. His money. Melinda spending his money. He had had too much to drink, and the film had been shitty, and he couldn't resist having a pop at her about her weight while he was on a roll. She was an easy target, too large to miss. And she was a champion bitch - in the super-heavyweight division.

She had fled upstairs, sobbing quietly. He had turned back to the movie and poured himself another glass of wine.

The "Beaver" in Barry "Beaver" Sullivan was not a self-honorary title. He had been given it at High School when he had been a buffed Adonis with thick luscious hair, an athlete's physique and a libido like any other teenage boy stuck in a boys' school next to a girls' school. Separated only by a hole-ridden chain-link fence between the sports pitches, and a rickety gate behind the bin area where the smokers and graffiti artists gathered.

And the shaggers.

Male and female.

It had always intrigued Barry that many people - many boys anyway - saw girls as conquests, targets to be acquired; primary, yet passive, objects in the pursuit of finding a repository for teenage ejaculate. Barry's starting assumption - which had proved presciently bang-on - was that it took two to tango and hormones did not discriminate on the grounds of gender. There was as much oestrogen wafting across the hockey field as there was testosterone raging on the rugby pitch.

With this in mind he had confidently preened and posed along the fence whenever any sporting occasion allowed and, as a result, secured the admiration of many of the senior girls (and some not so senior) and found himself with his hands often sticky and his cock often fondled. Home runs with the senior hockey eleven had been numerous and Beaver became *numero fucking uno* in the poundtown stakes.

His studies in female anatomy led him to muse on the idea of joining the medical profession but he was promptly cured of his disillusion when he saw the extent of the studies and years of dedication required to reach even junior Doctor status. Inborn bone-idleness and a piercing intelligence did the rest. He realised he need only rip out the few chapters on teeth from the burgeoning shelf of medical textbooks in order to specialise in dentistry. The only consideration had then been whether he would be able to stomach the idea of spending each day peering into the halitosis'ed caverns of rotting gums that yawned beneath the hairy noses and spotty complexions of unhealthy Scottish patients. When he had the good fortune to connect with a busty blonde dental technician who took a shine to him, dentistry had a new convert and his name was Barry Sullivan.

Throughout his twenties and into his thirties, Barry hit on anything in a skirt. Persistent and methodical - with practised ease - he smoothly screwed his way through the young and healthy female population of southern Scotland.

But his dentistry started to suffer.

And, possibly worse than this, he started to harbour something which he had never encountered before.

Doubt.

A very unusual state of affairs which troubled him deeply and would have given him sleepless nights - if he'd had any nights alone in which to catch some sleep. But he had pondered on it, long and hard, and came to the astonishing conclusion that what he needed, what he was sensing, what he was missing, was stability. He needed to settle down. Get married.

An amazing conclusion, but there it was. Without realising it, he had been searching for happiness - albeit in the skimpy underwear of many, many women - but searching nonetheless. And not finding it. This insatiable thirst for new conquests had become a treadmill from which he could not escape.

Except by stepping off.

The conviction had struck him forcibly and clearly and he was in absolutely no doubt that marriage was his solution.

But, boy, had he been wrong.

Melinda Forrest had been a gorgeous, vivacious brunette when he first saw her. Iridescent in a nightclub under the black light, she had shimmered and shone and given him a blowjob while he fingered her in the end cubicle. They had dated, moved in together, got engaged and then married in a whirlwind three months and she was pregnant with their first child before their first year together was up.

Barry couldn't have been happier.

At first.

Two more kids later he was wondering what had hit him.

Melinda had ballooned from a voluptuous size twelve to a gargantuan twenty-two, with stretch marks that looked like a contour map of the Cairngorms and a pussy like a wizard's sleeve. Barry had stared into a future offering eternal stability, security and the warmth of a family environment and realised that what stared back at him was an endless hell of sameness, familiarity and soul-crushing routine.

Divorce would ruin him; fidelity would kill him. Something inside Barry fell on its side and he realised that he had made a massive - *massive* - mistake. As quickly as he had persuaded himself that marriage was the solution he had had a Damascene conversion and now reverted to his original life-affirming philosophy of skirt-chasing.

He had just omitted to tell Melinda.

But while she might have been fat, she wasn't stupid. Barry had not exactly been subtle. Melinda didn't have the energy or self-confidence to do anything other than accept it for what it was. For now. Her life was her three young children and all her focus was devoted to them. But she would get around to disentangling herself from his wretched womanising when she had regained her energy and vitality. Meanwhile she could enjoy herself, and his money, distracting herself from his infidelity by excessive consumption.

Barry took this air of detachment as tacit approval. She no longer had any sexual interest in him. Well, *right back at you, fatso.* Life was short.

And he had an old nickname to live up to.

"Hello. Janine, is it?" The thin, pallid woman had an *I-want-to-see-the-manager* haircut. She was wearing white crocs and a pale blue tunic, buttoned to the neck, over dark blue slacks. Janine guessed they were elasticated at the waist. The woman held out her hand. "I'm Alison. Welcome to our little world."

Oh. My. God. Janine wanted to barf. So lame. Our little world!?! WTF? And crocs? She hoped against hope that what Alison was wearing was not a uniform she would be required to adopt. Ugh. White plastic clogs with strategically placed holes in them? Those holes - that was where your dignity leaked out. And those trousers made from fun-repellent material? Janine wasn't having any of that. She did not intend to start filling her basket in the *I've-given-up-caring* shop just yet, thank you very much.

Alison led her through to a small office off to one side

and closed the oak-veneered door. The stillness was soggy, squatting heavily over everything. Whilst Janine had been sitting in reception waiting, she had noticed this odd sensation - unable to quite locate it. Now, in this little cubbyhole of a room, it revealed itself to her. The whole place was hushed but loud at the same time. As if the very silence converted the slightest sound into a massive echo resonating around a vast dental cathedral.

"I thought I'd spend some time taking you through basic information and general rules, stuff like that. Then, once we've got that out of the way, I've got a few forms I need you to fill in - Health & Safety, Personnel, Payroll, Next of Kin - and then I'll give you a tour of the place. Won't take long." She smiled an apologetic crease of her lips, showing no teeth, dipping her head down to the left as she did so, like a poorly-coordinated Disneyworld animatronic. "Would you like a cup of tea?"

"Do you have any Doctor Pepper?"

"No." That smile again. "Tea. Coffee. Or water."

"I'm fine, thanks." Janine fiddled with the handbag in her lap and wished she had bought a bottle of something fizzy on her walk from the bus stop. This might be a long day.

"Okay. Well..." Alison smoothed her hands down her tunic, picked up a clipboard from the desk and clicked a ballpoint smoothly with her right hand. "Let's get started shall we?"

Janine sat silently as her induction into the particulars and peculiarities of Peebles Dental Surgery began. She rapidly tuned out and watched in a disembodied fashion as Alison pattered on about core working hours, annual leave, calling in sick, out of hours cover, yada yada. It was just like being back in Mr Jeffries' English class when he was banging on about Othello's anguish or something. As the droning continued, Janine belatedly realised there would be no bell to end the period today. That was last week. Last week she had been a student in High School. A young adult, as the Rector kept calling her and the other kids. This - *this* - was the world of work.

Oh God, what had she done? Maybe her pastoral teacher had been right about studying hard after all. This was looking grim. She screwed her eyes up slightly and examined Alison's face with a coroner's scrutiny. She was honest and straight, no doubt, but she also seemed somewhat efficient and cold. Maybe butter wouldn't melt in her mouth, but it probably wouldn't melt anywhere else on her either.

She let the talk wash over her and waited for the blessed relief of her first working lunch-hour when she could escape the looming suffocation by wall-to-wall carpet.

Julia pulled open a drawer and ran her eyes over the selection of underwear she had to choose from. Her mind wandered helplessly. Barry had a suavity and sophistication which her husband lacked. It aroused her simply by its novelty. And his sheer attention to her - just little things: brushing her arm here, stroking a stray tendril of hair off her face there - were a world away from the seeming indifference and casual slobbiness of her husband. Barry had subtlety and he was erudite. Paul had all the subtlety of a water cannon and probably thought erudite was a type of glue.

Barry had chatted admiringly, fawned almost. And made it quite clear that he desired her. Wanted her. Found her irresistible. Her ego had blossomed under his gaze and she found herself feeling newly sexy. When he had proposed dinner at a hotel she had known exactly what it meant. Felt the lack of passion from Paul like a raw wound. And wounds won't heal if they are neglected.

Barry wouldn't neglect her. He would bathe and stroke and attend. He had a magic touch. She smiled inwardly as she picked out a pair of briefs and placed them gently in her overnight bag.

Scantio removum.

Magic indeed.

FIVE

Barry's father had been an on-course bookmaker all his life until he had a heart attack at 61, during the 3:15pm at Kempton. All bets taken were declared null and void.

Throughout his formative years, from the time he was able to add up and scribble numbers down, Barry's father had dragooned him into the family firm and, until puberty and girls had intervened, Barry had loved it. The thrill, the excitement, even the downmarket smells of greasy food and unwashed punters, stale fivers and oily coins couldn't detract from the feeling that, when you were at a racecourse, you were at the centre of a maelstrom of wonder and power, galloping beasts making the ground tremble so that a handful of men (his father, hopefully, included) could put dinner on the table every night.

This hunger for the thrill and the chase had never left him and since segueing into the world of dentistry, he had used his familiarity and experience of horse-racing as a guide to help him structure and manage his off-course activities with the fillies.

So, Barry's process worked like this:

1. Studying the form: As any keen race-goer would know, the form-book was all. You can only judge a horse by the races it's won and Barry believed in research and attention to detail. He checked all new patients registered and perused his appointment list daily with a keen eye. When a new name showed up, he made sure he had some time spare to review the patient's file.

2. In the paddock: this was really the only random part of the process and was truly organic as far as Barry was concerned. He was a dentist and he saw 20-odd patients each day. All it took was one of them to be an attractive married women, in her twenties or thirties or forties, and the gleam in his eye lit up like an overhead examination light. He watched them move, watched them smile, saw how they engaged with him and how comfortable they were in his environment. Like being led around the ring by stable hands, their legs and their backsides, their sashays and their swaying, all gave clues as to their flexibility and suitability in the sack. When he was confident he had a good bet, he moved in.

3. Placing a bet: Smarm and charm offensive. Nothing too obvious at first, a light brush of an arm, compliments, a glint of a smile and a warm conversational interest in the woman herself. Very often they lit up at the slightest sign of flirtatiousness from him. Too many of these women seemed to be in loveless marriages themselves, with husbands who took them for granted and paid them no attention. Barry kept himself in shape. And he had lovely hair and teeth.

4. Going down: This was the riskiest part of the venture because, until this had been accomplished, he was fully exposed as a potential sex pest. And he had to ensure that his partner was, above all, willing. He would propose a second appointment, one always scheduled at 5pm. The end of surgery. Normal appointments ran until 4.45pm so that, by 5pm, everything was finished and he could close down, go home, finish off or attend to non-clinical admin and the like. Professional development he liked to think of it. Setting himself up ready for 5pm gave him something to look forward to and, once the patient was back in the chair, he would move in unambiguously and assess the welcome that awaited him. Sometimes it was downright hostility but most times it was uncertainty and a coy reluctance followed by a tentative engagement and then full-blown enthusiasm. He rarely had full-on sex in his surgery - the lighting was far too harsh - but getting to first or second base was all that was needed to gain agreement to move to the next phase.

5. Under starter's orders: He would meet them in the lobby bar, have a drink, put them at their ease before taking them to his room. Barry had a standard, recurring room booking at the Double Tree Hilton hotel, at Edinburgh airport which had served him well over the years. Airport hotels were used to one-night bookings, short notice, cancellations and delays, and frequent attendance by business travellers. To the uninitiated, Barry looked like all of these. If his partner was ill at ease about being detected she could even get the tram to the Park'n'Ride. Barry had thought of everything.

6. They're off! His regular room was 107, chosen because it was a disabled room with an extra-large shower/wet room, with strategically placed handles and grip bars for extra acrobatic support (and a pull chain in emergency, just in case something got out of hand!). The bedroom was large and spacious without being ostentatious and the large TV positioned on the bureau opposite the end of the bed, had a black bevelled trim on which it was child's play to conceal a small video camera which, *in situ*, was essentially invisible if you weren't looking and, if you were, looked like an innocuous infra-red receiver or mini-smart box that hotels used to control TV access. Nothing out of the ordinary to the untrained eye. In fact, once Barry had forgotten it and left it in place by mistake until the following week's booking and it was still there, untouched, its recording still in place on the tiny memory card which lived inside. The video it recorded may not be cinema-quality but it was HD and, whilst it lacked decent sound, it was entirely sufficient for his purposes. The pictures were worth a thousand words.

7. The winner's enclosure: The morning afterwards was usually an awkward time. His sexual prowess meant that his filly would certainly have enjoyed their time together - he'd never had a disappointed customer - but the cold light of day and sobriety often brought regret, lip-biting and nervousness about what had transpired plus how to get home. This was either the time when the wife realised her excuse had not been as carefully planned and prepared as she'd thought; or that the night had been so enjoyable - reminding a mature woman what good sex could be like outside a stale marital bed - that there were further shenanigans initiated upon waking. Barry would take a view at the end of the night and determine whether to rise early and disappear before she woke up, or risk an early morning quickie. If the latter, this would usually be followed by a stilted goodbye and a lift to some drop-off point. Barry always used swift checkout to minimise any awkward walk of shame through reception in the morning. He was, he thought, consideration itself.

8. Out to pasture: As the number of his willing mounts grew, so he needed to pay closer attention to maintaining the best performers and retiring the also-rans. When the novelty wore off, for him, he needed to be ready to engineer a break-up. Smoothly. Breaking up successfully was like knocking over a Coke machine: you didn't do it with one push, you had to rock it back and forwards a few times. Build momentum. Barry was always alert, listening to his dick, prepared to start the process at the first sign of boredom. The has-beens were put out to pasture as efficiently as he could manage, while he scouted for newly registered patients to replace them.

9. Managing his stable: More frequently, alas, it was fear, reticence, shame or guilt which caused his winners to want out. Just as he listened to his dick, he also listened to his gut. And sometimes he swore he could tell the end was coming. Maybe it was after just a one-night stand, or perhaps a two-or-three night affair, and there were some who kept it up for much longer. But inevitably a point would come where the lucky woman would say "Enough!". Because her husband was starting to suspect, or people were starting to talk, or she was feeling dirty and used, missing the reciprocity of love. This was where the video camera came in. Yes, he could use it for the purposes of his own entertainment - committing his best performances to the record for later, repeat viewing. And, yes, he did do this from time to time - no shame in revelling in your own excellence, Barry thought. But managing a stable meant using a little bit of carrot, a little bit of stick. And when the carrots no longer kept the fillies compliant, the stick came in handy. *Now, what would a husband say if he saw a video of his wife cavorting with another man? Surely, we don't want to get to that point, do we? Hmm? Precisely. So, how's Tuesday looking for you?*

Whatever the reason, whenever it arrived, Barry stood ready. No horse's head in the bed required. He had a much simpler offer the women couldn't refuse. And, after all these years of successful stable management, Barry wasn't at all sure whether this might not be the bit he actually enjoyed most.

The morning light filtered through the floor-length net curtains at the window and Julia woke blearily, momentarily confused as to where she was. Remembering with a jolt, she looked down at herself and rolled her eyes right to see if Barry was awake.

She was alone.

Appalled, confused and scared in equal measure she sat up in bed and looked around the room. Her clothes were scattered all around and she was still wearing a white suspender belt and one stocking. Nothing else. The champagne bottle was upended in the ice bucket. Slowly, she became aware that there was nothing in the room to indicate that Barry had ever been there. Her mind recoiled.

Was this, perhaps, intentional? To minimise any chance of her being found out? No trace of their assignation, no evidence that it had ever taken place? She wondered if she had dreamt the whole thing.

Or was it, perhaps, an indication that she had simply been used? Discarded, now that he had got what he wanted? Not even the human decency to go through the morning-after "Hello"s, "How was it for you?", "I'll call you"s and "It's not me, it's you".

She wasn't sure, and neither at this point would have surprised her. Relieved, nevertheless, she got up and walked round the room and the bathroom, checking. Truly, there was no mark of any kind to show she had not been alone the entire time. No wet towel, only one champagne flute, no used toiletries, abandoned cufflinks, or discarded condom wrappers. Wait! Had he used a condom? Disgusted with herself, now, she realised that not only could she not remember, she hadn't noticed because she hadn't cared. Her only thoughts had been her selfish pleasure and the feeling of getting some kind of bizarre revenge on Paul by engaging in this deceit.

She showered, turning the temperature as hot as she could bear, trying to sear the memories aware, slough away the skin that shamed her, and burn into her mind a plan as to what she should do now, how she should behave, what she should say to anyone about where she'd been, and what she'd done.

Sometime later, sitting on the hotel bed swathed in a white towelling robe, Julia dialled and tried to stay composed. Her thoughts were ricocheting but the only conclusion had been clear to her. She needed to speak to Barry and tell him she'd made a stupid, stupid mistake.

"Hello, dental surgery." The same sing-song tone as every other time Julia called.

"Hello, yes. I'd like to arrange an appointment please? With Mr Sullivan?"

"Can I take your name please?"

"Yes, it's Julia McInnes."

"Date of birth?"

"12.3.78"

"Right, Mrs McInnes. When were you thinking of?"

"Any day. This week. The sooner the better."

"Oh. Is it an emergency?"

"Yes. Yes, it is." Julia swallowed hard. "Do you have anything at 5pm?"

Somewhere near Cringletie farm, along what used to be the Cross Borders Drove Road and which was now little more than a muddy sheep-trodden path, Cullen sat on the wet grass with his back to a dry-stone wall.

His feet hurt and his mouth hurt and he was annoyed.

Annoyed because gone were the days when he could eat up twenty miles walking without noticing it. Age can do that to you. Whilst fifty wasn't exactly old, it's not exactly young either. He made a reluctant mental note to try and dial back his expectation of the miles he could manage in a day and moved on to the next annoyance: the damage Archie's cheese had wrought on his mouth.

He'd rooted through the medical kit in his rucksack and found nothing that suited. His nearest stash of tools, medicines or emergency supplies was even further away and, dammit, his feet hurt. He felt gingerly along his gum line with one grimy finger and, encountering tenderness, he winced. A line from an old movie sprang unbidden into his head - *A man's got to know his limitations* - and an image of his wife standing over him appeared suddenly out of nowhere and he wondered what she would say if she were still alive. *Stop being a big baby and get it sorted,* she'd have said. Of course she would. He smiled at the thought.

With a deep sigh, he pushed himself up from his sitting position and started walking along the Drove Road to Peebles.

"What delivery?"

"Flooring." Paul said, waving vaguely at an imaginary pallet full of wooden planks. Julia couldn't see them either, as she was on the other end of the phone.

"Flooring?"

"Yeah. Mitchell's delivering at 5.00. Or 5.30. Or something."

"Or something?" Julia was beyond exasperated. "What does that mean?"

"Last thing, s'what it means. They close at 5.30 and this is the last delivery off their lorry."

"So when will it be exactly?"

"Five-ish."

"Paul, I said exactly."

"Yeah, five-ish." This, for Paul, was just about as exact as anyone should reasonably require.

"I have a dental appointment at five."

"Right." Paul acknowledged this in a tone which indicated the information she was providing was interesting but ultimately irrelevant.

"What I mean is, I can't guarantee I'll be here for this delivery. Can't they just leave it on the drive?"

"Well yeah, they can. But I don't want six hundred quid's worth of oak flooring left out where any Ned can half-inch it. I should be back by then, touch wood."

"Touch wood? Is that some kind of joke?"

"No, just sayin' that with a following wind an' that, I'll be home in time. Just lettin' you know, is all."

"Paul, I have to go to the dentist. It's important!"

"Is it?"

"Yes."

"Why?"

Julia felt a cold sweat rising to meet a hot flush descending. Her stomach knotted and she blinked furiously. "Because... I have had to cancel and rearrange this bloody appointment so many times now, all because you can't be here when you're supposed to be!" She had started the sentence off flustered and panicked that she might be giving herself away, but ended it triumphantly with the tables turned and the pressure placed directly on him for his lack of punctuality and track record to prove it. Paul caved.

"Look, I'll be there alright? Just make sure that delivery doesn't take place unattended."

"You'll be here?" She knew he wouldn't.

"Promise." He definitely wouldn't.

"Great." Julia hung up.

Now she was stuck. She'd have to rearrange her appointment. Another day wouldn't hurt would it? Or perhaps the longer she left communications with Barry the worse this would get. What if he had notions of an affair, or romance? She took a deep breath. Calm yourself, woman. You don't want to confront Barry in his surgery anyway, do you? What sort of madness is that? Leave him a note. Arrange to meet somewhere discrete, away from Peebles. Not the hotel again, definitely not there. Somewhere else.

Think.

She rang the surgery to cancel her appointment and then went in search of a pen and paper.

SIX

Janine put down her emery board with a sigh and answered the phone on her headset.

"Good afternoon, Dental Surgery."

It was half-past two and already she was losing her bright-and-breezy telephone manner. Whether the callers could detect her boredom she could neither say nor find it in herself to care. If her vocabulary had stretched to encompass the word *ennui* she would have recognised it at once, clasped it to her bosom, and vowed to use it daily hereafter. Only halfway through her first week and the awful emptiness of an afternoon's double geography stretching before her now seemed a lot more attractive than she had ever thought possible.

And hidden, below the desk, was the crowning insult to this ordeal. Worse than the boredom; worse than the petty rules and regulations; worse than the endless forms; worse than everything else. She wriggled her toes in the pair of white crocs Alison had given her and winced at the total and utter indignity.

She glanced over to the photocopier, half-hidden at the back of the admin office. Alison was there now, flapping at the touch-panel like an albino sea-lion typing an angry email, eyes only for the tiny screen on the machine currently telling her there was a paper jam.

Somewhere.

Janine sighed again and turned back to the PC showing

the telephone control panel. The Office Manager was a smart, prim, rail-thin woman with a face like haunted tupperware. Her dark brown hair was cropped close to her scalp and she had a tendency to move her head in snatches as she talked, her neck jerking out then back in, making her look like a startled bird, on the alert for the neighbour's cat, ready to fly at a moment's notice. Ever since her welcome on Monday, and her orientation and training, Alison had been hovering round Janine like a cloud of midges at a water treatment works.

And she was cold. Oh, so cold. Her pinched face was Tippex white, her eyes pregnancy-test blue, her lips the colour of an angry bruise. And to denote her seniority, inside the collar of her pale buttoned-up tunic she wore a chiffon scarf the colour of a DUI urine sample. Maths had never been Janine's strong point but she reckoned Alison was 50% puritan, 50% sergeant-major and 75% passive-aggressive control-freak.

"Above all else, Janine." Alison had reassured her. "Don't worry about making mistakes. It is your first week of your first ever job. We all make mistakes. Making mistakes is how we learn. And you will find I have no problem with mistakes, providing you learn from those mistakes and don't repeat them. It takes time to become familiar with a new role and develop the skills you need to do well in a job. And time needs patience. Fortunately, I have the patience of a saint."

Yes, thought Janine, if we're talking about Saint Fuck-Me-I'm-A-Hypocrite.

"One day, if you apply yourself determinedly, you could be a Senior Receptionist." Alison had smiled, intending encouragement - probably - but delivering menace. By the end of orientation, Janine had no more ambition of becoming a Senior Receptionist than she had of becoming a drugs mule. She put her right hand to her headset, pushing the speaker more firmly to her ear. The connection sounded like they were calling from a toaster on a submarine.

"Hello? Dental Surgery. Can I help you?"

Nothing but static and a decrepit whisper. Ha! Janine thought, it's the hoarse whisperer!

"Hello."

Janine jumped in her seat as a man's voice, rich and deep came not from the headset but from the other side of the glass screen in front of her. She looked up from the computer into the speckled grey eyes of a tall man wearing a damp leather cowboy hat, a dripping waterproof which had seen better days, and a lined and weatherbeaten face bearing a grimace. He had both hands splayed on the counter, nails short and trimmed, his fingers like those of an old man, wrinkled and hairy. She blinked, confused, and then hearing nothing more through the headset, cut the connection and flicked the sliding screen door open to talk directly to this old man.

"Can I help you?" She tried on a smile, hoping it would fit.

"I need to see a dentist."

"Which one?"

"Any one."

"Sorry, I mean which dentist are you registered with?"

"I'm not registered."

"Oh." Janine's face fell. Her first new registration and she had quite, quite, forgotten the procedure. Alison had led her through it on Monday but the information graft had failed to take and now, a whole day and a half later, all that was left was something about a form. She glanced over to the photocopier but the angry email was no nearer completion. Janine decided to take an executive decision. She pulled up the appointment diaries of the two dentists on duty today and scrolled briefly through them.

The dental intercom briefly buzzed into life, the sound suddenly filling reception: *Helen Masters, Surgery 3 please.*

"Name?"

"Cullen."

"Date of birth?"

"Look, I just want to see a dentist."

"Mr Cullen, I need your date of birth."

"Why?"

Janine blinked and sat back in her chair. She didn't know the answer to the man's question and now wondered what the answer actually was. She stalled for time.

"Address?"

"Look. Can I see a dentist today or not?"

"Mr Cullen..." Janine, finished scrolling through the diary and found nothing.

"It's an emergency." The man grimaced and ran his tongue over the teeth behind his top lip.

"I'm sorry, I-"

"Please?" His probing tongue struck tenderness and he winced.

Janine looked into his sad eyes and felt herself yield. She could see that there were no empty slots left this afternoon. All appointments, fifteen minutes apart, were showing solid blue - meaning each patient had been contacted earlier that day or the day before and had confirmed their attendance. She scrolled down to the white emptiness on the calendar which started at 5pm. Next to Barry Sullivan's name was a winking asterisk.

Janine hovered her mouse over it and a pop-up window appeared showing a 5pm slot with the name Julia McInnes in green italics with a strikethrough.

"All we have, Mr Cullen, is a 5pm with Mr Sullivan. Is that too late for you?"

"I'll wait." And, with that, the man withdrew from the desk, and sank down on a chair in the corner. Like some kind of electronic device, he appeared to freeze, his gaze locking on the middle distance and an invisible silence immediately surrounding him. Janine looked askance again at the clock and then back to the man, realising he was planning on sitting there for the next two hours.

She watched him for a short while but when he showed no sign of returning her look, she turned back to her screen and waited for the phone to ring once more.

Barry was closing his laptop lid when the door opened and a tall cowboy strode in. Barry's boner fell.

"Can I help you?"

"Cullen. 5 o'clock." The man surveyed the room and moved towards the dentist chair without prompting.

"I, er, wasn't expecting... I mean, I wasn't aware that I had any more appointments for today. Would you mind if I just check briefly?"

"They've gone."

"Who?"

"The girls at reception. The last one was putting her coat on when she asked me to come through."

"Ah, I see. Well, er, this is most irregular. Mr, ahm..?" Barry peered the the computer screen on the desk away to his right which his assistant used. She, too, had left early believing the diary was done for the day.

"Cullen."

"Yes, well you see Mr Cullen-"

"Just Cullen."

"What? Ok. Whatever." Barry didn't have the time or patience for this right now. Where the fuck was Julia? That's what the diary had said. He'd been looking forward to this all day. "You see, Cullen. My assistant has gone home and I am unable to perform any treatment single-handedly so if you could just make a new -"

"You're a dentist aren't you?"

"Well, yes, of course."

"Then dent!"

"Mr Cullen, I really-"

"It's just Cullen." The man was as calm as you like but there was steel in his eyes and the set of his jaw. His voice was quiet and soft but Barry found himself held by it, vice-like. "I have been in pain for 48 hours and I have been waiting outside all afternoon for my 5 o'clock appointment. It is now 5 o'clock - ten past actually. I am here, you are here. I have a pain in my mouth, you are a dentist. I see no reason why we can't just get this done, here and now."

"As I have tried to explain Mis-, ah, Cullen, my assistant has left for the day. It is she who prepares anaesthetic needles, sterilises my instruments, records my actions and notes, and so on and so forth. Without her, well, I'm afraid you might experience some pain which would be unnecessary and, well, painful." Barry gave a wan smile and ran his tongue over his front teeth as if to emphasise the issue at stake.

Cullen sat forward in the dentist chair and gazed into Barry's eyes, his face mere centimetres away. "I am experiencing pain now. If I have to experience a little more in order for this pain to go away, I will happily do so. That would be preferable than spending another 24 hours with this pain right now." He looked askance at Barry. "Do I need to sign some form? A waiver or something? Is that it?"

"No, no. That won't be necessary."

"Good. Ready when you are." Cullen leant back in the chair, raised his face towards the ceiling and threw open his mouth.

Barry, realising that this man was not going to shift and could well become agitated if pressed further, decided that discretion was the better part of valour. And besides, he thought, as he selected a clean pick, put on a new pair of surgical gloves and manoeuvred the light over his pliant patient's mouth, the man didn't want pain relief! This might actually be fun.

Alison Fairbright was patient. She could do patient exceedingly well. And efficient. Patient and efficient: these two strengths had served her so diligently over the years. Wherever would she be without them?

Patience was a virtue and she knew all about virtue, having kept hers intact for many, many years. Her dutiful approach to work had taken precedence over everything else for most of her life. She'd been busy working hard, doing her utmost for this company or that boss. Slaving away, ignoring idle distractions like personal relationships. Until one day she looked up and realised she had missed the "here, have a boyfriend" meeting and was staring lonely middle-age in the face.

Lonely middle-age had stared right back at her, and Alison had blinked first.

She had tried online dating and found it full of men who were awful, predatory or just unsanitary. From their photos alone, many of them looked the sort who would turn up at a sex trial just to bang on the van. So when she had taken the job at the Dental Practice, Barry had wafted into her life like a dream incarnate. A vision of class and style lacking all but the white charger.

And patience. Unlike herself, Barry normally had all the patience of a wounded wasp that had spent twenty minutes on hold. But she forgave him - because she understood. He had often taken time out of his busy day to talk to her, reveal his inner turmoil and the troubles with his marriage. With Melinda for a wife, why - he had shown the patience of a saint to put up with it for as long as he had!

So here was her golden opportunity. A marvellous man with talent, looks, money and prestige. And all that she needed was patience. His marriage couldn't last forever. Meanwhile she focussed on keeping the dental practice running like a well-oiled machine. How could he fail to value her, not notice her worth to the practice? To him?

She didn't bother herself with those mindless, squawking gossips on reception. What did they know? She knew her Barry. If he did have a roving eye - *if* - that was all it was. Harmless flirting, at best. She was his intended, perfect life partner and she could feel it in her bones.

And so, daily, she waited. Patiently.

SEVEN

Barry leant back on the dental stool and watched the finished video with some satisfaction. And a sizeable erection. He'd read the note Julia had left at reception after the cowboy had gone, and his gut had twitched. It told him she wanted out and he found himself not entirely surprised. But she had been quite, quite spectacular in bed, and he wasn't about to let a little reticence stop him from enjoying many more sessions like that one. Oh no. Here was where the fun really started.

Stable management procedures: engaged.

An old hand at this, it had taken him less than an hour to edit down the raw footage into something usable which he could put on a cheap memory stick. He wasn't making a cinema feature here, just needed a few basic clips, each clearly showing Julia's face and body, while she engaged in obvious and unambiguous sexual activities with him. All he needed were the highlights, topped and tailed by a head-and-shoulders piece to camera which he would do now in his surgery.

He liked to see if he could get his videos to be exactly fifteen minutes long - he had long forgotten why that was; presumably because the first one he ever did had been exactly that long, by coincidence, and he liked the symmetry of them all being the same. As he pulled his stool closer to the counter and positioned his webcam ready to start recording his bit to camera, he looked across to the shelf containing all his previous blackmail tapes. Ever considerate of longevity he had copied them all to DVD in HD quality and filed them carefully on a CD rack on the shelf above his squash trophies and medical certificates. Cognisant of the need to keep them from prying eyes he had chosen to hide them in plain view, here in his surgery, rather than somewhere at home where his ever-expanding wife might accidentally stumble across them. To ensure no-one like Alison ever looked at them he had carefully labelled the spines of the jewel cases with stickers which read Tax Returns, Receipts & Invoices, and so on.

Smiling, he checked his reflection in the webcam image on his laptop screen and pressed record.

"Hello, Julia." He began.

The package dropped onto the doormat and Julia somehow sensed that, whatever it was, it wasn't good news. Something about the *pher-lap* sound it made. She put down her handbag, picked up the padded envelope and ripped it open. There was no return address, no note inside. Just a small USB stick. Nothing else.

Julia instinctively felt afraid. She didn't want to look at it, or touch it. But she couldn't not. Her heart beat in her chest like a fist. Something about the antiseptic, cold colours of the stick - a body of baby blue with a cover of translucent white - told her this was from Barry.

Normally she'd have missed the postman, rushing off to work. Today she was a tad late but now, despite herself, she knew she'd be even later. She wasn't going to be able to do any work today until she knew what was on this thing. The problem was, she had no way of seeing what was on it without leaving a digital trace. She didn't know much about computers, but she knew that much. The battered laptop she shared with Paul sat on the kitchen worktop, from where she checked their email, facebook, the usual. No way was she inserting this stick into that.

She had cheated on Paul and felt sick. That was bad enough. She hadn't figured out what to do about that - yet - short of deciding to tell Barry that it had been a one-off. No-one must know. Especially Paul. And if he were to find out? And from his own laptop?

Was this Barry's response to her note? What did he have to say that he couldn't say to her face? How could she find out without looking at what was on it? She needed to find a way to check the contents without Paul finding out.

Julia waggled the stick in her hand and paced the length of the hallway. Up and down, up and down. Agitated and afraid, guilty and ashamed, her mind was abuzz. At the very moment she needed to most, she found herself completely unable to think straight.

The Chambers Cafe lies on the floor below the library in the Chambers Institute building on Peebles High Street. Library patrons are allowed to take books down the backstairs and read them at tables or in the sofas and armchairs that dot the large carpetted area in front of the coffee desk - as long as they return them back upstairs and don't waltz out of the front door with them and out onto the street.

Cullen sat nursing a pot of tea while waiting for the pelting rain to stop drumming against the windows to his right. On a small table for two in the farthest corner of the room, he had reassigned the other chair to a different table and sat hunched on one elbow, earphones jammed into his ears, stirring his tea listlessly with a plastic stirrer.

His mouth hurt still after his visit to the dentist, but in a more natural wounded way, rather than the raw unceasing pain which had gnawed its way through his lower face for the previous few days. His jaw itself felt bruised and battered, which it probably would be given the amount of force the dentist had applied in extracting the tooth - almost sitting astride him at one point in order to gain the necessary amount of purchase. Cullen couldn't avoid the feeling that, given the dentist's triumphant look as they parted, Sullivan had enjoyed himself a little more than was appropriate. An ember of anger flared briefly and then evaporated when he suddenly heard someone say "Hello, Julia."

He looked up and around only to see no-one. The voice continued briefly, clear and deep, then stopped in mid-sentence. It was a man's voice.

Sullivan's voice.

Coming through his earphones.

The second row of seats in the library, last cubicle on the left, was where Julia sat nervously tapping the USB stick against her glossy thumbnail and jiggling the shoe on her left foot on and off, her legs crossed under the desk. This was it.

No-one knew she was here, apart from Jennifer on the front desk. There were no internet cafes in Peebles but here in the public library you could buy an hour on a computer for £1, as long as you filled out a basic form with your name, address and scribbled a signature at the bottom.

She had slunk into the slot furthest away from anyone else and now sat staring at the grey monitor with the green light winking at her in the bottom bezel. She feared that the minute she touched the mouse the screen would spring into life, and a loud bing-bong Windows welcome tone would greet her. She reached for the volume control knob on the desktop speakers and turned it off.

Taking a deep breath, she grasped the mouse and entered the username and password Jennifer had given her. She inserted the USB stick into one of the front sockets and sat frozen, waiting for a window to open. When it did it showed one file only on the stick - a video. Julia felt a knife in her throat. Heart pounding, she clasped both hands in her lap and looked down at them, seeking some sign of comfort or peace. None came.

Head still down, she slowly scanned the room, lifting her eyes beneath her fringe to see if anyone was watching her; if anyone could see her screen. Like a child in a church pew, she slowly raised her eyes to the multi-coloured icon and double-clicked. Another window opened on a black screen with a play timeline at the bottom reading 14:45 and the cursor started to move. The black dissolved into a smiling head-and-shoulders shot of Barry Sullivan sitting in his blue scrubs, his head halo'ed by the bright surgery room lights behind him. He started talking but there was no sound.

Julia reached for the volume control and twiddled it. Barry continued on blithely, trundling along, smiling confidently in silence. Then she realised she had turned the speakers off so as not to be greeted by the login tune. Sweating now, she pressed the On button and, again, twisted the knob left and right trying to hear what he was saying. Still there was no sound!

Cullen put his head down and sat motionless as if any movement on his part would prevent him from hearing the voice again. Sullivan's speech was snatching on and off; there would be a gap, then his voice would return, louder for a few words then growing quieter before being cut off again. Cullen listened intently until the volume spiked suddenly and he yanked the buds from his ears and held them at arm's length until he could tell that the sound had faded. Tentatively he held one bud to his ear and heard Sullivan's greeting again: "Hello, Julia."

This time the volume stayed steady and he listened for another minute or so until Sullivan's voice stopped and was replaced by eager moaning and groaning. The audio quality was poor but this was undeniably the sound of two, or possibly more, people engaged in sexual activity of some kind. Cullen reddened, scraped his chair back to stand and shoved the offending earphones into his coat pocket.

Julia had wrenched the controls like a mad fool, dragging the cursor back to the beginning of the timeline and hitting play again. Still no sound. No static, nothing - even when she bent her head straining towards the speakers. She sat, appalled, as Barry mouthed silently to her and then the scene cut to a close-up of an untidy double bed and a naked couple writhing upon it. Recognising herself at once, she frantically closed the video window and jabbed the power button on the PC, shutting it off. Sick and slick with sweat, she pulled the

USB stick from the slot and sat shaking. Her jaw and hands were clenched tight and she jammed her eyes shut trying not to cry. Cry: with anger at her own stupidity; rage at her lack of self-discipline and the jeopardy she had now placed her marriage in; shame at herself for submitting and succumbing to the overtures of a man who now clearly showed himself to have the moral compass of a greasy, effervescent turd

And beneath the rage, just the slightest curiosity as to why Barry had not bothered with sound. If this was an attempt at blackmail he surely wasn't relying on sign language or his skills at mime, was he?

Jennifer watched as the tall man in the cowboy hat approached the enquiry desk from the backstairs. He was holding a pair of tangled earbuds in his hands and, as he placed them on the desk between them, his knuckles shone white.

"These are... yours." He seemed unsure quite what to say. "Your colleague lent me them to listen to an audiobook on one of the PCs? I've just been down to the cafe and forgot to return them. Sorry."

"Oh, right. Thanks." She swept them up from the counter and crouched down trying to find a home for the earbuds in a drawer. Cullen looked down at the register on the table, a list of names of those who had booked out the library computers. The name beneath his own was Julia McInnes.

"These are those new bluetooth ones aren't they?" Jennifer said as she stood to her feet. "Do they work ok?

"Work?" Her question had seemed to wake him.

"Yes. I mean, you know clarity? Range? These wireless

things, they're not supposed to be as good quality as wired headphones are they? And I have no idea how far you can be from the sound source before they cut out. Although, if you're just sitting at a PC that's not really an issue is it?" She smiled politely.

"Yes. Fine, yes." He looked at her squarely. "The range is excellent."

PART THREE

NOTHING BUT THE TRUTH

EIGHT

Cullen pulled up the collar on his waterproof against the wind, crammed his hat more firmly down and headed over towards the bus stop. The only other occupant of the shelter when he got there was the receptionist who had waved him into his appointment two days before.

She was sitting hunched, head down, threading the fingers on one hand through the fingers of the other, over and over. Every now and then she gave a tiny sniff. Cullen stood away stiffly to one side. When she looked up and saw him, she'd been crying.

"Oh, hello again." The girl wiped a snotty nose on a wet woollen sleeve and attempted to dab her eyes dry with one cuff of a jumper under her coat. "Mr... Cullen, isn't it? Did Mr Sullivan fix your tooth?"

Cullen silently dug his hand into his pocket and retrieved a greying hankie, spattered with dried blood, and unveiled its cargo.

"Ugh!" The girl recoiled and searched his eyes keenly. "Are you ok? That looks like it... might have hurt a smidge?" She tried on a smile of encouragement.

"Better out than in." Cullen ran his tongue across the wounded gap in his teeth again, tasting imaginary blood.

"That's unusual." She looked puzzled. "They're supposed to avoid having to do an extraction, you know? Did he not offer you any alternative treatment?"

"No." Cullen considered this information for a

moment. "It was an emergency."

"What's that got to do with it?"

"Dunno. Cost me too. Emergency fee."

"What? There's no such thing!"

Cullen scrutinised her face. "No?"

"No." Janine protested. "He's just a bloody robber and sadist. As well as a sex pest!" This last phrase was spat out with real venom and she immediately burst into tears again, covering her face with her hands.

Cullen remained rigid for a few seconds, unsure how to respond. In the end, he moved closer and sat down next to her, wanting to - but afraid to - put his arm around her. She looked terribly young. He was wondering quite what to say when she spoke up, saving him the job.

"I'm sorry." She sniffed. "He's such a bastard."

"The dentist?"

"Yes, Barry bastard Sullivan. Barry bloody bastard Sullivan. Barry bloody bastard beaver Sullivan!"

"Beaver?"

"Yes." She stifled a laugh. "It's his nickname. Pathetic isn't it?"

"Beaver?" Cullen frowned. "Builds dams or something?"

"What?" It was her turn to screw her face up, her tears forgotten.

"Chews pencils?"

"Beaver! You know..." she waved her hand with a flourish over her lap. "Women."

"I don't..."

"Never mind." She wiped her nose on her sleeve again and looked at Cullen smartly. "He likes women. A lot."

"I see."

"Too much."

Cullen raised one eyebrow but remained silent.

"Except me." She crossed her arms. "He fired me."

"Because he doesn't like you?" Cullen was struggling to stay on the rails of this youngster's train of thought.

"He fired me because I don't like him!" She jutted her chin out. "Or, should I say, I don't fancy him as much as he fancies himself."

Cullen thought for a moment. "Is that a job requirement then?"

"Oh yes! And agreeing to blow him."

"Blow...?"

"You know!" She made a strange gesture, rocking a small fist in front of her mouth while simultaneously poking her tongue into her cheek.

"Ah."

"Yes, ah. I told him to fuck off."

"Right." Cullen nodded.

"So he fired me."

She burst into tears and Cullen looked uncomfortably up the road for any signs of an impending bus.

"I'm going to tell my Dad. He'll have his guts for garters."

"Is that wise?"

"Wise? Who the fuck cares? Wise! He's sacked me and I've not even been there a week. I have rights you know."

"Yes. But as an employee with such a short time in the role -"

"Fuck off!" Janine swung her small handbag at him. "I made your appointment - remember?" Cullen's tongue unconsciously reached for the hole in his gum again. "Next morning, he told me off. Said I shouldn't have done it. I told him it was actually my job to make appointments. He said this was... different. 5 o'clock appointments are different. Apparently. How the fuck am I supposed to know? Said he'd forget all about it if I... you know." She made the strange gesture again and wiped her nose with a tissue. "Ha, I bet he was surprised to see you in his 5pm slot! Serves the fucker right."

"What do you mean?"

"You're not his 5pm type." She looked him up and down, smiling. "Wrong sex for a start. That's his beaver slot."

Cullen eyed her, interested. "His beaver slot?"

"Aye. And you wouldn't have got it at all if Mrs McInnes hadn't cancelled at such short notice."

"McInnes? Would that be Julia McInnes?"

"Yeah. She was next up, I reckon. Can't keep his hands to himself or his dick in his pants. Fucker!"

"Ok." Cullen straightened in his seat, checked to see there was still no bus on the horizon, and then bent towards Janine, speaking quietly. "What can you tell me about Barry Sullivan?"

Janine jiggled the keys in the door to the dental surgery and tiptoed in, waiting until Cullen had fully entered behind her before locking the door again. Cullen turned all the lights in reception on.

"What are you doing?" She squawked. "Someone will see us!"

"And? You work here - as far as anyone else knows - and you've every right to come back to the office at..." he consulted the clock on the wall "5.40pm, to retrieve something or whatever. Perfectly legitimate and nothing to act surreptitiously about."

"Surrep-what?"

"-Titious. Furtive." Her face still drew a blank. "Sneaky?"

"Well, yes actually." Janine nodded. "I've been fired, remember? I'm not supposed to still have these keys."

"Well, can you show me a list of all the people who have had 5pm appointments with Sullivan in the past few months? Then we can leave."

"In for a penny." Janine sighed, turned the desktop PC on and waited for it to go through its startup motions. When she logged on and brought up the calendar list of appointments it showed six different names in the past three months. All women.

"Can I see the patient details for these women?"

"Erm... well, no. That's not allowed actually." Christ, hark at her! She sounded just like Alison. "Patient confidentiality, you see. What are you looking for?" She peered at him, beneath her damp fringe.

"Well. Answer me one thing. I don't want to see their details. Just tell me if they are married or not."

Janine eyed him suspiciously and then tapped away at the keyboard for a minute, scrolling and searching. "Done."

"And?"

"No, now you tell me why you're doing this. Then I'll tell you if they're married or not."

"Hmm." Cullen looked half-annoyed, half-admiringly at this slip of a girl, capably standing her ground. "Sullivan certainly met his match when he hired you didn't he?"

"Technically, he didn't hire me. Alison did." She smirked. "But, well, compliment accepted."

"Ok." Cullen started ticking off the fingers on his right hand. "Firstly, he harassed you and then fired you. That's not... nice. And it's not right. Second, I'm going to bet that all of these women are married?" He looked at Janine for any indication that he was right but she raised an eyebrow and folded her arms. He continued. "I bet they are and I further bet that he has been blackmailing some, perhaps all, of these women into having sex with him. And if they don't, he threatens to tell their husbands. Which is also not right."

"Or nice."

"Or nice." It was his turn to raise an eyebrow. "Does that mean they are married?"

"All of 'em."

"Ok. So, I think it is time our Mr Sullivan was taught how to tell right from wrong."

"Hmm. Any other reason you're doing this?"

Cullen pushed his tongue gingerly once more into his wounded gum, then looked her in the eye. "No."

Janine considered this for a moment. "Ok. So, what now?"

"Now? You show me how you make 5pm appointments."

"What time did you say?" Julia whipped her neck around to face Paul. She stopped chopping the onion and froze, waiting for his answer. Paul was casually unloading himself from his overalls and hanging them up by the door. He looked vainly for his slippers.

"Five."

"PM?" Julia felt her heart stop.

"What do you think?" Paul asked, searching under the sofa. "Have you seen my slippers?"

"5pm. Tomorrow?"

"Yes." Paul was becoming slightly irritated, distracted

from his slipper search. "Where're the dogs?"

"In the back garden." Julia replied on auto-pilot. She willed herself to calm down but felt the blood pounding in her throat. "Who with?"

"I don't know." Paul was not a regular dentist-goer and didn't actually care who he saw or didn't see, as long as he was able to experience a pain-free visit. He opened the back door and his two terriers rushed to meet him. "Somerville, is it? Summerfield? Summat anyway." He knelt down to be submerged under soggy dogs. "Hey fellas! How's it going, huh? Miss me?"

"Sullivan?"

"Prob'ly."

The gulf between how concerned Julia now was and how unconcerned Paul appeared could not have been wider. Her fate was sealed. Barry had obviously decided to not only go through with some kind of blackmail, but seemed intent on doing so straight away. She quickly reviewed the four options she could see:

1. Prevent Paul making the appointment. Perhaps this wasn't needed as his natural unreliability meant he'd probably miss it, or forget it, if simply left to his own devices.

2. Rearrange his appointment to buy her more time.

3. Try and contact Barry before Paul's appointment and see what she could do, if anything, to stay his hand.

4. Come clean and 'fess up to Paul and take the consequences. Perhaps all would be forgiven? She looked at him as he rough-housed with his dogs, his hands like meathooks. He had never hit her, but there was always a first time. Or maybe he'd hit Barry! That would be helpful. Or not. Ok option 4 was her last - *last* - resort.

"You ok?"

She glanced over to see Paul looking up at her, one eye squinting into the sunlight shining low in through the kitchen window. "Yes. Fine, fine. Just remembering I need to make myself an appointment."

"Didn't you just have one the other day?"

"I did." She snapped instantly back to indignation. "I cancelled it so that I'd be here for your bloody delivery, didn't I?"

"Oh." She swore sometimes Paul lived off-planet. "You didn't need to do that. I told you I'd be back in time."

She looked daggers at him. "But you weren't."

"Wasn't I?"

"No."

"Oh." He stood up, his dogs entertained enough for now. "Soz." He sauntered over to the fridge, took out a cold beer, twisted the top of the bottle and flipped it into the sink with practised ease.

"Can you put those in the bin please? Where they belong?" Julia snapped.

"Soz." Paul leant into the sink, snatched the bottle top up and dropped it into the swing bin. "Again." He muttered under his breath and shuffled off to the lounge.

Julia stood frozen at the worktop, gazing at nothing out of the kitchen window. After a while, she looked down at the knife in her hands, the onion skins on the chopping board, the sound of the fan in the warming oven, the familiar homeliness of this little scene.

And silently began to cry.

NINE

Jake sat in reception. Today was his tenth wedding anniversary and he had bought his wife, Susan, a gift. These last twelve months had been something of a rollercoaster in their marriage. He had had an affair and Susan had been on the verge of finding out when he came clean and admitted it. She had thrown him out for a fortnight and then he had managed to crawl back into the house and start the slow, slow process of rebuilding trust and rekindling the love that had been there all along, lying forgotten and unnoticed. They had managed to keep it from their children, he believed, although Susan had told her best friends about it (she'd later informed him). A year of reconstructing their marriage and, whilst they weren't completely out of the woods, they had talked and talked, reignited their passions for each other and his past behaviour now only re-emerged in fleeting and rare occasions when a random word or scene on a TV show would remind her of it and there would be an immediate and noticeable temperature drop. A real tumbleweed moment where Jake would hold his breath and hide his eyes, waiting to deploy the right word or gesture to smooth them over this hump and put the needle back into the groove.

He watched the clock hands tick around towards 5pm and worried the eternity ring box in his jacket pocket.

Davy was genuinely pissed off. He threw his coat and scarf on and bustled out of the office, stalking head-down over the river Tweed to the surgery. He hated going to the dentists, retaining a deep fear of them which he had harboured since childhood. Combined with sensitive teeth and receding gums, he lived in particular fear of the water-pick they used to remove tartar and other buildup on his teeth. Every time he went he asked them to use the old steel scraper jobby, and every time he allowed the dentist to persuade him that it would be ok and there really wouldn't be any discomfort. And every time, the dentist would be right: there'd be no discomfort - just a shitload of pain. Searing bolts of nerve-cold would shred their way into him and he'd dig his rigid fingers into the arms of the chair and stiffen his legs, bracing himself for the next shot of agony. And if he ever needed a filling - oh man, the injection! Feeling the penetrating needle and the icy novocaine squirrelling into his gum. His jaw would ache for days afterwards, whether from real or imagined bruising he could never tell. Even when the dentist had extended the time between check-ups from twelve to eighteen months, these visits still came around too frequently.

Jean, his wife, would have told him not to be a big baby and to man up, but he had never let on that this was a big deal for him - he didn't need the ridicule or sympathy or comment. He might tell her one day but sharing wasn't really his thing. His view on life was very simple: you found a partner, moved in, got married and that was that. Life's mission was complete and you could then get on with your career and stuff. It was all straightforward and he couldn't understand why others made everything so complicated. When colleagues at work would bemoan their own relationship troubles, Davy would smile and trot out a little anecdote of his own. Some time ago, when they'd been married about three years, Jean had asked him where he thought their relationship was going. He'd just laughed at her and said "Going? It's not going anywhere. It's arrived!". She'd never mentioned it again. Other marriages might be pairings of incompatible souls but he and Jean were both on the same page.

He swept into the dental practice reception wearing a mask of grim determination.

Tony paced up and down outside the dentist's gulping down the last of his cigarette. He didn't have any more gum on him so if the dentist complained about his breath he could go fuck himself. Cheryl was always banging on about it to him as well - not his breath so much as the stench on his clothing and in his hair. Plus his stubble and dirty nails. God, she could go on. Usually took a good belt around the ears to shut her up. Or a smack on the back of the head. Nothing that would show. No need to make it anyone else's business, was there?

He stubbed his cigarette out in the metal ashtray attached to the wall below the window and lit another.

Julia stood in front of the wardrobe mirror shaking, both arms held tightly across her chest. She'd been so fucking stupid. The minute hand on the clock ticked round to 5pm and she realised she'd better get her skates on. She opened the suitcase on the bed and started to pack.

Barry pulled his last pair of latex gloves from the dispenser and snapped them on, checking his appointments screen as he did so. Wendy had been dismissed, it was 5pm and his final assignation for the day was... Cullen? That couldn't be right. He scrolled across to check the notes against the appointment, assuming another mistake by the newly-fired Janine.

On cue, the man himself walked into the surgery and Barry exploded at him. "Mr Cullen! I told you last time that simple etiquette requires you to wait until your name is called before entering my surge-. What are you doing?"

Cullen had closed the door behind him and snicked the lock into place. He turned menacingly back to Barry, his eyes hard and cold. "Time we had a wee chat." He said, stepping towards the dentist chair.

Barry pushed his own stool back towards the window, its castors spinning on the polished floor. He quickly scanned the room for a way out, or a means to defend himself - his visitor's intentions now alarming him. He saw Cullen, too, cast his eyes around the room as if looking for something and then move over to the computer on the counter top. While he fiddled with something, Barry seized his moment and grabbed for the catch on the window behind him. He struggled with it between the vertical blinds but managed to free it and push the lever up, swinging the window ajar. As he pushed his weight down on his stool ready to launch himself at this novel escape route he felt an arm around his throat and he shot back across the room, hurtling on screaming wheels, coming to rest only when his face crumpled into the all-too-solid hydraulic lift of the dentist chair. Barry put one hand to his mashed face and tasted blood.

Cullen picked him up like a cold bag of loose giblets and tossed him into the dentist chair, swinging the instrument tray across Barry's body in one smooth move, trapping him in place.

"Talk."

Barry probed his teeth with his tongue, delicately checking for damage. He grimaced as he did so, eyes warily looking up at Cullen beneath a bloodied brow. For a moment the pair locked eyes, silently weighing each other up. Barry broke his gaze away first and tried to push one index finger into his mouth. Cullen grabbed at it and pinned it to the arm of the chair.

"Talk."

"Mngh mmng mnwn." Blood dribbled from his lips and down his chin.

"Spit." Cullen nodded to the faucet and spittoon. Like an obedient patient, Barry tentatively leant over and spat into the shining drain.

"Rinse." Cullen nodded. "Good dental hygiene."

Barry swigged the pink mouthwash, swooshed then spat before Cullen thrust him back down into the chair

"Right. Now, talk."

"About what?" Barry wiped his mouth with the back of one hand, recovering a little composure. "This is assault, you know? I'm going to prosecute you for this."

"Really?" Cullen looked amused, his eyes glistening. He leant his face right into Barry's and growled: "Tell me about Julia McInnes."

Barry frowned. He'd thought this lunatic was exacting some kind of revenge for his rough-handling of his tooth pain the other day. "What?"

"Julia McInnes."

"What about her?"

"Tell me about her." Cullen swung the overhead armature above Barry's head and shone the lights right into his eyes. "And the others."

"What others? I don't know what you're talking about." He blinked rapidly, his breath ragged. He could smell the sweat of his attacker and see all the stubble and pores in his face.

"Yeah you do." Cullen reached behind Barry, out of sight, and when he brought his hand back into view it was holding the dental drill. The tiny motor whined into life.

Jake was the first to tune into the conversation being broadcast over the intercom. He cocked an ear and caught the eye of Davy in the process. The pair smiled, embarrassed, and then both listened to the two men's voices - one low and calm, the other higher and much more tense - until they heard the names of their respective wives mentioned and their smiles promptly dropped. When Tony sauntered in and saw two blokes gawping with their heads tilted, Jake put a finger up to his lips and looked at him.

"Fuck off!" Tony glared. "Don't shush me, you fucking-" He stopped short when he heard Cheryl's name being spoken by the higher pitched voice.

The more this man fed names to him, the more Barry warmed to his theme. He had no idea what Cullen's game was, and he was going to make sure the police threw the book at him when he managed to get free from his current predicament, but he found himself unable to resist this golden opportunity to brag about his conquests. He realised he'd never had anyone he could share this information with before and now he had a captive audience - even if it was himself who was currently playing the role of captive.

"Nice piece of skirt, that Cheryl. Everything in good working order, if you know what I mean. Don't look at me like that! Nothing wrong ... two consenting adults. No-one else's fucking business. Certainly not yours." Barry raised his eyebrows meaningfully. "Got a lovely little tattoo of a dolphin. Just above her pubic hair line. Well, I say pubic hair. She doesn't really go in for that much, if you catch my meaning. Suits me - I like a clean work surface."

There was a sudden series of banging noises that shook the floor, and a gathering rumpus that quickly culminated in the surgery door being violently hammered from the other side. Barry tore his face from Cullen's and looked anxiously towards the door. The lock held for mere seconds and when the door flew open there was a large furious man standing in the doorway, with two more red faces peering from behind his bulk. Realising that, perhaps, it was better the devil you knew than the devil you didn't, Barry turned back to seek reassurance from Cullen, but his former assailant was nowhere to be seen. The only other movement in the room came from the vertical blinds swaying erratically in the open window.

Big Paul pulled into the car park in his white van and exhaled with a groan. The clock on his dashboard said 17:32 and he figured he'd missed his appointment, but he clambered from his van and walked over towards reception. A tall figure in a cowboy hat appeared from between some bushes and came towards him, pocketing his phone. Paul looked askance and picked up his pace.

"Surgery's closed." Said the stranger.

"Huh." Paul shrugged. "Light's still on."

"Cleaner."

"Is that right?" Paul attempted to push past the man and got a distinctly off-colour whiff of something as he did so. "Guess I'll just double-check, as I'm here."

"I... wouldn't."

"I've got an appointment." Paul winced. "Had an appointment. 5pm. Bit late, I guess."

The man stood his ground as a number of sirens keened in the night, swiftly followed by a police car which fishtailed around the corner in the snow and skidded to a halt outside the dentists. Two patrolmen got out just as an ambulance hustled into view from the other end of the street, pulling to a stop alongside the police car.

The blue lights strobed the two men as they stood watching.

"What's happened?" Paul wondered, out loud.

"Whatever it was, you missed it."

After a while one of the policeman reappeared, scanning the car park and street as he returned to his car. The man in the cowboy hat turned to go and nudged Paul as he did so. "Come on. Don't want to be mistaken for witnesses, do we?"

Paul looked at the man with interest, seeing something in his face. What was it: honesty? Concern? "Not a fan of Old Bill then?" Paul asked.

"Not... as a rule." The man smiled thinly.

"Me neither."

They walked back to Paul's van in silence, the man still giving off a strong unpleasant odour. Paul wondered if it was the chemical element, Ew. There was the sound of frantic scuffling and barking emanating from the back of his van.

"Well." The man checked out the livery on the van and smiled to himself. Blowing on his hands, he rubbed them together. "Haven't you got a wife and a home to go to?"

"Yeah." Paul looked at the man, searching his eyes. "Yes, I do."

"I'd do that then."

Paul pulled the van doors open and Penn and Teller shot out and immediately laid siege to the man, jumping up at him, scratching his jacket arms and rucksack. The man leant forward to pet Teller and then looked up at Paul.

"Your dogs eat cheese?"

"Eat anything."

"It's just that I read somewhere that cheese makes some dogs sick."

Paul shrugged. "If it does, they'll eat that 'n'all."

The man slung off his pack and reached inside. He pulled out a somewhat-squashed, large grey cylinder which was leaking pale cheese from substantial wounds in its sides. Paul realised this was the source of the man's stench.

"Stinking Bishop." The man offered the wheel to Paul who just nodded to put it at his feet for his dogs.

"Whiffs a bit. Any good?"

"Weapons-grade, you might say." He lay the cheese on the floor and watched for a moment as the two dogs devoured it. "Name's Cullen."

Paul shook the offered hand. "Paul. Mate's call me Beep."

"Beep?"

"Short for BP. Short for Big Paul." He smiled, a touch

embarrassed. The man just gave a small nod.

"Nice to meet you, Beep. Mind how you go."

Paul watched as the man gave his hat a small adjustment, almost by way of a farewell, and then turned and strode off into the shadows. When he was out of sight, Paul turned back with his dogs and sauntered over to the policeman who was calmly talking into his radio.

TEN

Julia was standing, frozen, at the end of the bed, the suitcase in front of her piled with random items she had thrown in. She couldn't decide who was to blame for the pickle in which she found herself - Barry or Paul - but it certainly wasn't her. Oh no.

And even if it was, there was no point dwelling on it. She could almost hear Paul now: "Don't keep blaming yourself." He'd joke. "Just blame yourself, then move on."

Paul.

The sound of the front door opening jerked her awake and she panicked, jamming the suitcase closed and shoving it under the bed. Heart thumping in her chest, she looked at herself in the mirror, dabbed at her eyes with a tissue from the bedside table and smoothed her dress down with both hands. Taking a long, slow breath she set her jaw, straightened her back and strode out onto the landing.

Paul was shambling up the stairs, shaking his head.

"Murder." He sighed heavily and raised his eyes, catching Julia's worried look.

"Murder?" Julia felt goosebumps rise and her legs start to buckle. She reached for the bannister to steady herself.

"Fuck, aye." Paul let out another heavy sigh and ran his thick fingers across his bald spot. "You ok, babe?"

"Oh my God!" Julia one hand to her mouth, her eyes filling up. She felt her whole weight sag into the newel post. "Paul, what have you done?"

"Me? Ain't done nothing." Paul reached out to catch her, startled, but Julia's eyes flared and she backed away. "Everybody ruining it for everybody else, is what it is."

Julia stared at him, horrified. "What? What everybody else? Who?"

Paul's brow furrowed. "S'not my fault." He cast his eyes down and shuffled past her into the bedroom.

"Paul!" Julia grabbed his shoulder and wheeled his bulk round to face her. "What have you done? Look at me!"

Paul couldn't meet her gaze and stood, cowed, a man-child in front of her. "I missed my appointment."

She lifted his chin and then took a step back, searching his eyes. She didn't know what to say.

"I was late, ok?" Paul sulked. "Murder on the bypass. Bloody rush hour traffic. Didn't get there 'til half-past." He pulled his mouth into a small grimace. "I'm sorry. Really."

"What?"

"I'm sorry, alright?"

"You were late?" Julia felt relief flooding into her but wouldn't allow it full rein until she had more information.

"Yes." Paul's shoulders slumped again. "Soz."

"You were late." A statement, no longer a question. Goosepimples rose on her arms and neck.

"Aye." Paul dropped his hands and headed back into the bedroom, already starting to put his ignominy behind him. "Might have to see another dentist next time, mind!" He added, somewhat brightly, as he rooted through the wardrobe.

"What? Why?" Julia found herself waggling her head from side to side, trying to shake her thoughts into some sensible structure.

"Sunderland's had some kind of accident. Attacked or something. 'S what the copper said."

"You mean Sullivan?" Julia played with the stray curls at the base of her bob. "Barry Sullivan, the dentist?"

"Aye." Paul came back out onto the landing, casually wiping his nose with the back of a sleeve. "With his own instruments too! Neat, huh? Someone decided he'd been getting too friendly with one of his patients. Went all Marathon Man on him."

"Marathon Man?" Julia screwed her face up.

"Yeah. Is it safe? All that." Paul smiled at her, broadly. "Seems they eschewed anaesthetic 'n all."

"I'm sorry?"

"Esch-ewed." Paul enunciated deliberately. "Good word, innit? Means didn't bother with, apparently." He beamed again. "Looked it up on my phone. Coppers these days, huh? Getting some kind of education any road."

"Is he, erm, ok?" Julia didn't know what answer she wanted to hear but felt this was the question she needed to ask. She stood, swaying slightly, as if on the deck of a ship, while the world around her shifted and heaved. "The dentist?"

"I don't think so." Paul grinned. "Mouth ripped to shreds, face mashed to a pulp. Wasn't pretty. At all. Used the drill imaginatively, according to the copper."

"Why is it amusing?"

"Well, not amusing as such. Just that I'd heard a few stories - down the pub - about him, you know?" Paul looked at her, innocently. "Heard he liked diddling married women on the side."

"Really? Well, then. He deserved it, didn't he?" She looked at her husband, as if for the first time, and drank him all in. She cast her eyes over his strong shoulders, arms and hands, his trunk and solid stance; scanned his face and his innocent, trusting smile. And when she had finished, Paul standing there silently and slightly clueless while she did all this, Julia moved into his arms and squeezed him tightly round his midriff.

"Me and you." She said, into his chest.

"You and me." Paul replied, ruffling her hair.

"Lots and lots."

"For us to see."

"You and me."

"Me and you."

"Lots and lots."

"For us to do."

"Hey." Paul pulled himself away slightly and tilted her face up so he could look into her eyes. "I promise I will never ever be late again." He cradled her face in his meaty hands, thumbs brushing the tears away. "Ever."

"Yeah." Julia sniffed and smiled. "You will."

"I am not a fun sponge!" Alison protested, simultaneously indignant and confused as she was having to guess at what this new term implied.

Janine smiled. "Ok. If you say so." They were sitting back in Alison's office, once more going through the sheaves of forms and questionnaires required to be completed for all new employees. "It was my Dad's words, not mine." She lied. "I didn't ask him to write that letter, you know? I was upset and really - really - angry about being fired. I wanted to do something to complain but also wanted to wait until I wasn't so upset. He sort of took it on himself, you know?" She gave another apologetic smile. "Guess I've always been his little princess."

"What is a fun sponge anyway?"

"It doesn't matter. Can we drop it and start again? Please?"

Alison's world was still rocking from the revelations that were coming out about Barry. They had started as murmurings, and then she had begun the process of piecing things together. But once she found his 'tax returns' and viewed one - she could not bring herself to do more - she had handed them over to the police. In the days since then she had been operating in a kind of zombie mode, keeping things in the surgery moving, ensuring appointments were rearranged and starting the process of recruiting an additional dentist for the practice. There was plenty to do and she was able to keep busy. Until it was time to go home.

She spent her evenings hugging herself and tearing into box after box of tissues, her dreams in pieces. She wasn't experienced in the ways of love, had had only a few relationships - but she knew what men were like. She'd thought Barry was different.

What a stupid fool she'd been.

And then, beyond how he had hurt her, she had looked, appalled, at the stuff he had done to others. And the letter from Janine's Dad had touched a raw nerve. The realisation that her inability, or unwillingness, to see what had been going on around her, brought her to tears. She had called Janine immediately and asked her to come back in for a chat and, if she wanted, to resume her position as Junior Receptionist.

"Yes, we can start again." Alison reassured her. "I just want to make sure that we are both clear on how things should proceed and that we are both happy that a line has been drawn under this whole affair. I mean, business. A solid red line."

"I understand. And I agree."

"You will need to agree that, in the world of work, you have a lot to learn Janine. And while you are clearly a bright and capable girl, there are rules and procedures that need to be followed."

"I get it."

"Procedures which are there for a reason. Which help things run smoothly and which predate your arrival. Procedures which all other members of staff understand and are happy to adhere to."

"Yes."

"Procedures such as not arranging appointments for other patients in calendars above and beyond your pay grade."

"I'm sorry."

"Such as not gaining access to the premises once all other staff have left for the day."

"Yes."

"Or allowing non-members of staff to access patients' confidential files."

"I didn't let him!" Janine bristled. "I specifically told him he could not see that sort of stuff."

"Good." Alison brightened. "And if you wish to query any procedures, or even suggest improvements. Why, we have a Staff Suggestion procedure for just that very thing!"

"Does it have a form that needs to be filled out?"

"Of course."

"Right." Janine swallowed. "Ok. I shall... keep that in mind."

"Excellent." Alison smiled. "We will see you first thing tomorrow then."

"Do I need to wear the crocs?" Janine tried on a smile

she thought might suggest hope more than desperation.

It didn't.

Alison pursed her lips and then gave a long, deep sigh. "Let's... think about that, shall we?"

POSTSCRIPT

Barry Sullivan lost all his teeth and was unable to afford a whole mouth dental implant after his wife, Melinda, filed for divorce on the grounds of serial infidelity and her lawyers took him to the cleaners. He retired from dentistry and is currently trying to build a second career as a motivational speaker. He has a new book out called *Happiness is a Worn Gum.*

Alison Fairbright decided to forswear men and devote her life to the optimisation of procedures and processes within the field of dental clinic administration. At a conference on How To Get ISO Certification for Dental Clinics she met a fellow Office Manager called Malcolm who is a stickler for process and a devotee of all the acronyms which make the lives of business administrators so fascinating. They have a second date next Tuesday.

Janine Crombie still works at the Peebles Dental Practice and was recently promoted to Receptionist Assistant (Grade 3) after Alison introduced formalised job and salary grades in order to qualify for the Investors In People (IIP) commendation now adorning the wall in reception. Janine received a pay rise of £0.50 per hour and was, obviously, thrilled.

Julia McInnes devoted herself newly to the nurture and

regeneration of her marriage to Paul. Confident in their new-found togetherness, she persists in believing that - one day - Paul will turn up on time.

Paul McInnes, along with his dogs Penn and Teller, developed a liking for strong cheese. He did not renew his missed dental appointment and has not been to the dentist again. He bumps into Cullen more often than you might think, usually while out walking his dogs.

Mungo James Cullen lives alone. Somewhere. When the weather is cold, his jaw still bothers him.

AUTHOR'S NOTE

This is my first attempt at a novella and I would like to thank Claire, for giving me the belief and push to get it started. I could have done it without her, but probably wouldn't have. Also for her many constructive comments and insightful feedback on reading my early drafts.

My thanks, once again, to Big Paul for allowing me to depict him unrealistically. He won't read this either (prob'ly) and wouldn't want my thanks anyway. He'd much rather have a good bottle of Scotch - but this is cheaper.

Peebles does not have a dental clinic like the one I depict, nor does the Chambers Institute have a cafe as I describe. Neither is there, at the time of writing, a cheese shop on the High Street. Don't really know why I set the story there, now I come to think of it. Lazy, I guess.

Any other inaccuracies or omissions are intentional and not meant to represent a lack of research or thoroughness on my part. Honest.

Finally, I'd like to extend no thanks at all to the concept that is NaNoWriMo (if you are not familiar with it, be grateful and endeavour to keep things that way). Whilst I was able to use the month of November to focus my efforts in writing this story, there the usefulness of the whole enterprise ends. My condolences to anyone who has ever tried to complete a novel in NaNoWriMo and I genuinely hope that you manage to succeed once you have recovered from the whole experience.

Bah humbug and Merry Christmas.

mjf
20.12.2017

Join the Cullen & Big Paul Fan Club!

If you enjoyed the adventures of Cullen and Big Paul, why not join their fan club? You'll get early notice of new books, special offers, a monthly newsletter from the author, unique free content, invitations for discounts and more!

JOIN at **download.markfarrer.com/signup**

Tell others what you thought...

If you enjoyed this book, please leave a review on Amazon

About the Author

You can learn more about Mark Farrer at **www.markfarrer.com** or follow him on Twitter **@mark_farrer.**

Printed in Great Britain
by Amazon

68758482R10068